IN VAIN

BY

HENRYK SIENKIEWICZ

Author of

QUO VADIS," "WITH FIRE AND SWORD," "THE DELUGE
"PAN MICHAEL," "HANIA," ETC.

TRANSLATED FROM THE POLISH

BY

JEREMIAH CURTIN

Fredonia Books
Amsterdam, The Netherlands

In Vain

by
Henryk Sienkiewicz

Translated by Jeremiah Curtin

ISBN: 1-4101-0320-X

Reprinted from the 1899 edition

Fredonia Books
Amsterdam, The Netherlands
http://www.fredoniabooks.com

In order to make original editions of historical works available to scholars at an economical price, this facsimile of the original edition of 1899 is reproduced from the best available copy and has been digitally enhanced to improve legibility, but the text remains unaltered to retain historical authenticity.

INTRODUCTORY.

"IN VAIN," the first literary work of Sienkiewicz, was written before he had passed the eigh-
teenth year of his life and while he was studying
at Warsaw.

Though not included in his collected works
by the author, this book will be received with
much favor; of this I feel certain.

The first book of the man who wrote "With
Fire and Sword" and "Quo Vadis" will interest
those of his admirers who live in America and
the British Empire. These people are counted
at present by millions.

This volume contains pictures of student life
drawn by a student who saw the life which he
describes in the following pages. This student
was a person of exceptional power and exceptional qualities, hence the value of that which
he gives us.

JEREMIAH CURTIN.

JERUSALEM, PALESTINE,
    March 8, 1899.

IN VAIN

❦

CHAPTER I

"AND this is Kieff!"

Thus spoke to himself a young man named
Yosef Shvarts, on entering the ancient city,
when, roused by toll-gate formalities, he saw
himself unexpectedly among buildings and
streets.

The heart quivered in him joyfully. He
was young, he was rushing forward to life; and
so he drew into his large lungs as much fresh
air as he could find place for, and repeated
with a gladsome smile, —

"And this is Kieff!"

The Jew's covered wagon rolled forward, jolt-
ing along on the prominent pavement stones.
It was painful to Shvarts to sit under the canvas,
so he directed the Jew to turn to the nearest
inn, while he himself walked along by the side
of the wagon.

1

Torrents of people, as is usual in a city, were moving in various directions; shops were glittering with a show of wares; carriages were passing one after another; merchants, generals, soldiers, beggars, monks pushed along before the eyes of the young man.

It was market-day, so the city had taken on the typical complexion of gatherings of that sort. There was nothing unconsidered there; no movement, no word seemed to be wasted. The merchant was going to his traffic, the official to his office, the criminal to deceit, — all were hastening on with some well-defined object; all pushed life forward, thinking of the morrow, hastening toward something. Above that uproar and movement was a burning atmosphere, and the sun was reflected in the gleaming panes of great edifices with just the same intensity as in any little cottage window.

"This uproar is life," thought Shvarts, who had never been in Kieff before, or in any large city.

And he was thinking how immensely distant was life in a little town from the broad scene of activity in a great city, when a well-known voice roused him from that meditation.

"Yosef, as God lives!"

Shvarts looked around, gazed some seconds at the man who called him by name; at last he opened his arms widely, and exclaimed, —

"As God lives, it is Gustav!"

Gustav was a man small and thin, about twenty-three years of age; long hair of a chestnut color fell almost to his shoulders; his short reddish mustache cut even with his lip made him seem older than he was in reality.

"What art thou doing, Yosef? Why hast thou come? To the University, hast thou not?"

"Yes."

"Well done. Life is wretched for the man without knowledge," said Gustav, as he panted. "What course wilt thou choose?"

"I cannot tell yet; I will see and decide."

"Think over it carefully. I have been here a year now, and have had a chance to look at things coolly. I regret much a choice made too hastily, but what is one to do afterward? Too late to turn back, to go on there is lack of power. It is easier to commit a folly than correct it. To-morrow I will go with thee to the University; meanwhile, if thou hast no lodgings, let the Jew take thy things to my room, it is not far from here. Thou mayst begin with me; when thou art tired of me, look for another man."

Yosef accepted Gustav's offer, and in a few moments they were in the narrow lodgings of the student.

"Ei, it is long since we have seen each other. We finished our school course a year ago," said Gustav, putting aside Yosef's small trunk and bundle. "A year is some time. What hast thou done this whole year?"

"I have been with my father, who would not let me come to the University."

"What harm could that be to him?"

"He was a good man, though ignorant — a blacksmith."

"But he has let thee come now?"

"He died."

"He did well," said Gustav, coughing. "The cursed asthma is tormenting me these six months. Dost wonder at my hard breathing? Thou too wilt breathe hard when thou hast bent over books as I have. Day after day without rest for a moment. And fight with poverty as one dog with another. — Hast money?"

"I have. I sold the house and property left by my father. I have two thousand rubles."

"Splendid! For thee that will be plenty. My position is poverty! Oh the cursed asthma!

Oi! that is true. One must learn. Barely a
little rest in the evening; the day at lectures,
the night at work. Not time enough for sleep.
That is the way with us. When thou enterest
our life, thou wilt see what a University is.
To-day I will take thee to the club, or simply
to the restaurant; thou must learn to know
our students immediately. To-day, right away
thou wilt go with me."

Gustav circled about the room without inter-
mission; he panted and coughed. To look at
his bent shoulders, sunken visage, and long
hair, one might have taken him rather for a
man tortured by joyous life than by labor; but
the printed volumes and manuscripts in piles,
the poverty in the furnishing of the room, gave
more proof than was needed to show that the
occupant belonged to that species of night birds
who wither away while bent over books, and die
thinking whether a certain syllable should or
should not be accented.

But Yosef breathed the atmosphere of the
chamber with full breast; for him that was a
world at once new and peculiar. "Who
knows," thought he, "what ideas are flashing
through the heads of dwellers in fourth and
fifth stories? Who knows what a future those
garrets are preparing for science?"

"Thou wilt make the acquaintance to-day of many of our fellows," said Gustav, drawing out from beneath his bed a one-legged samovar and putting a broken dish under it in place of the two other legs. "But let not this evening offend thee," continued the student, as he let charcoal drop into the samovar. "I will make tea. Let not heads partly crazy offend thee. When thou hast looked round about at the city, thou wilt discover that there is no lack of fools here as in other places; but it moves forward with no laggard steps. There is no lack among us of originals, though there is much that is empty and colorless. This last is ridiculous, and the dullest of all the stupidities. In some heads there are blazes of light, in other heads darkness like that out of doors at this moment."

Silence reigned for a time in the chamber; there was no noise there save that made by Gustav while puffing and blowing at the samovar. In fact, night had been coming gradually, on the walls and ceiling of the room an increasing darkness was falling; the fiery circle reflected from the samovar widened or narrowed as Gustav blew or stopped blowing. At last the water began to sound, to hiss, to sputter. Gustav lighted a candle.

"Here is tea for thee. I will go now to the lecture," continued he; "wait thou here, or better sleep on my bed. When thy time to pay money comes, thou wilt have also to look after lectures. The work is dreary, but there is no escape from it. Student life has its bitter side, but why mention this in advance? Our student world and the rest of society are entirely separate. People here neither like nor receive us, and we quarrel with all persons, even with one another. Oh, life here is difficult! If thou fall ill, no man, who is not a student, will reach a hand to thee. This is the fate of us poor fellows; moreover people are angry because we play no comedies, we call things by their names."

"Thou seest objects in black," remarked Yosef.

"Black or not black," answered Gustav, with bitterness, "thou wilt see. But I tell thee that thou wilt not rest on roses. Youth has both rights and demands. They will laugh in thy eyes at these rights, these demands; they will say that thou art not cooked enough, they will call thy wants exaltation. But devil take it, the name matters little if the thing it describes hurts or pains thee. As to that thou wilt see. — Pour tea for thyself, and lie down to rest. I shall be here in an hour; and now give me that hat, and good-by!"

For a while the panting, puffing, and steps of Gustav were heard on the stairway. Yosef was alone.

Those words of Gustav impressed his friend strangely. Yosef remembered him as different. To-day a certain disappointment and peevishness were heard in his voice, mental gloom of a certain kind broke through those words half interrupted, half sad. Formerly he had been healthy in mind and in body; to-day his breathing was difficult, in his movements and speech appeared wonderful feverishness, like that of a man who is exhausted.

"Has life tortured him that much already?" thought Yosef. "Then one must struggle here, go against the current somewhat; but this poor fellow had not the strength, it seems. A man must conquer in this place. It is clear that the world does not lay an over-light hand on us. Devil take it! the question is no easy one. Gustav is in some sort too misanthropic; he must exaggerate rather easily. But he is no idler and must go forward. Perhaps this is only a mask, the misanthropy, under which he finds his position more convenient and safer. But really, if one must take things by

storm or perish? Ha, then I will go through!"
exclaimed the young man, with strength,
though in this interjection there was more
resolution than passion.

An hour after this monologue panting was
heard on the stairway a second time, and
Gustav entered, or rather pushed in.

"Now follow!" cried he. "Thou art about
to enter the vortex of student life; to-day thou
wilt see its gladder aspect. But lose no
time!"

While speaking, he turned his cap in his
hand, and cast his eyes on every side; finally
he went to a small table, and taking a comb
began to arrange his long yellow, or rather
his long faded hair.

At last they went out to the street.

At that time in Kieff there were restaurants
where students assembled. Circumstances
were such that it was not possible to live
with the city society. Those various city
circles were unwilling to receive young persons whom the future alone was to form into
people. On the student side lack of steadi-
ness, violence of speech, insolence, and other
native traits usual to youth were not very
willing to bend themselves to social require-
ments; as to the country, that furnished its

social contingent only in winter, or during the time of the contracts. So the University was a body entirely confined to itself, living a life of books in the day, and leading a club life at night. For many reasons there was more good in this than evil, for though young men went into the world without polish, they had energy and were capable of action. Wearied and worn-out individuals were not found among them.

Our acquaintances passed through the street quickly, and turned toward the gleaming windows of a restaurant. Under the light of the moon it was possible to distinguish the broad, strong figure of Yosef near the bent shoulders and large head of Gustav. The latter hurried on in advance somewhat, conversing with Yosef or with himself; at last he halted under a window, seized the sill, and drawing himself up examined the interior carefully. Finally he dropped down, and said, while wiping off whitewash from his knees, —

"She is not there."

"Who is not there?"

"Either she has been there or she will not come."

"Who is she?"

"What o'clock is it?"

"Ten o'clock. Whom art thou looking for through the window?"

"The widow."

"The widow? Who is she?"

"I fear that she is sick."

"Is she thy acquaintance?"

"Evidently. If I did not know her I should not be occupied with her."

"Well, that is clear," answered Yosef. "Let us go in."

He raised the door-latch; they entered.

A smoky, hot atmosphere surrounded them. At some distance in the hall faces of various ages were visible. Amid clouds of smoke, which dimmed the light of the wall lamps, and outbursts of laughter, wandered the tones of a piano, as if wearied and indifferent. The piano was accompanied by a guitar, on which thrummed at intervals a tall, slender youth, with hair cut close to his skull and with scars on his face. He played with long fingers on the strings carelessly, fixed his great blue eyes on the ceiling, and was lost in meditation.

The person sitting at the piano had barely grown out of childhood. He had a milk-white complexion, dark hair combed toward the back of his head, sweetness on his red lips, and melancholy in his eyes. He was delicate, of a slight build of body, and good looking. It was evident that he had played a long time, for red spots on both cheeks showed great weariness.

With their backs to the light stood a number of men from the Pinsk region, all strong as oaks, and at the same time so eager for music of every sort given in the restaurant that they formed a circle around the player, drooped their heads, and listened with sighs or delight.

Other young fellows were on benches or in armchairs; a few tender girls, of the grass-hopper order who sing away a summer, circled here and there. It was noisy; goblets clinked in places. In the room next the hall some were playing cards madly, and through a half-open door the face of one player was visible. Just then he was lighting a cigar at a candle standing on the corner of a table, and the flame either smothered or rising for an instant shone on his sharply cut features.

The woman at the refreshment counter ex-amined near the light, with perfect indifference, the point of the pen with which she entered down daily sales; at her side, leaning on a table, slumbered her assistant in wondrous oblivion. A cat sitting on a corner of the counter opened his eyes at moments, and then closed them with an expression of philosophic calm and dignity.

Yosef cast a glance around the assembly.

" Ho! How art thou, Yosef?" called a number of voices.

"I am well. How are ye?"

" Hast come for good?"

" For good."

"I present him as a member of this respected society. Do thou on thy part know once for all the duty of coming here daily, and the privilege of never sleeping in human fashion," said Gustav.

"As a member? So much the better! Soon thou wilt hear a speech. — Hei, there, Augustinovich, begin!"

From that room of card-players came a young man with stooping shoulders and a head almost bald, ugly in appearance. He threw his cap on a table, and sitting in an armchair began, —

" Gentlemen! If ye will not remain quiet, I shall begin to speak learnedly, and I know, my dear fellows, that for you there is nothing on earth so offensive as learned discourses. In Jove's name! Silence, I say, silence! I shall begin to discourse learnedly."

Indeed, under the influence of the threat

silence reigned for a season. The speaker
looked around in triumph, and continued, —

"Gentlemen! If we have met here, we have
met to seek in rest itself the remembrance of
bitter moments. ["Very well."] Some one will
say that we meet here every night. ["Very
well."] I come here nightly, and I do not
dream of denying it; I do not deny, either,
that I am here on this occasion! [Applause;
the speaker brightens and continues.] Silence!
Were I forced to conclude that every effort of
mine which is directed toward giving a practical
turn to our meetings is shattered by general
frivolousness, for I can call it general ["You
can, you can!"], not directed by the current
of universal agreement which breaks up in its
very beginning ["Consider, gentlemen, in its
very beginning"] the uniform efforts of individuals — if efforts marked by the regular object of uniting disconnected thoughts into
some organic whole, will never issue from the
region of imagination to the more real field of
action, then, gentlemen, I am the first, and I
say that there are many others with me who
will agree to oppose the sense of the methods
of our existence so far [Applause], and will
take other methods ["Yes, yes!"] obliging, if
not all, at least the chosen ones [Applause]."

"What does this mean?" asked Yosef.

"A speech," answered Gustav, shrugging his shoulders.

"With what object?"

"But how does that concern any one?"

"What kind of person is he?"

"His name is Augustinovich. He has a good head, but at this moment he is drunk, his words are confused. He knows, however, what he wants, and, as God lives, he is right."

"What does he want?"

"That we should not meet here in vain, that our meetings should have some object. But those present laugh at the object and the speech. Of necessity the change would bring dissension into the freedom and repose which thus far have reigned in these meetings."

"And what object does Augustinovich wish to give them?"

"Literary, scientific."

"That would be well."

"I have told him that he is right. If some one else were to make the proposal, the thing would pass, perhaps."

"Well, but in his case."

"On everything that he touches he leaves traces of his own ridiculousness and humiliation. Have a care, Yosef! Thou in truth art not like him in anything so far as I know, but here any man's feet may slip, if not in one, in another way."

Gustav looked with misty eyes on Augustinovich, shrugged his shoulders, and continued, —

"Fate fixed itself wonderfully on that man. I tell thee that he is a collection of all the capacities, but he has little character. He has lofty desires, but his deeds are insignificant, an eternal dissension. There is no balance between his desires and his strength, hence he attains no result."

A number of Yosef's acquaintances approached; at the glass conversation grew general. Yosef inquired about the University.

"Do all the students live together?"

"Impossible," answered one of the Lithuanians. "There are people here of all the most varied conceptions, hence there are various coteries."

"That is bad."

"Not true! I admit unity as to certain higher objects; the unity of life in common is impossible, so there is no use in striving for it."

"But the German Universities?"

"In those are societies which live in them-

selves only. A life of feelings and thoughts,
at least among us, should agree with practice;
therefore dissension in feelings and thoughts
produces dissension in practice."

" Then will you never unite? "

" That, again, is something different. We
shall unite in the interest of the University, or
in that which concerns all. For that matter,
I think that the contradictions which appear
prove our vitality; they are a sign that we
live, feel, and think. In that is our unity;
that which separates unites us."

" Under what banner do you stand, then? "

" Labor and suffering. We have no dis-
tinguishing name. Those who are peasant
enthusiasts call us ' baker's apprentices.' "

" How so? "

" According to facts. Life will teach thee
what these mean. Each one of us tries to live
where there is a bakery, to become acquainted
with the baker, and gain credit with him.
That is our method; he trusts us. The ma-
jority of us eat nothing warm, but a cake
on credit thou wilt get as long as thou
wishest."

" That is pleasant! "

" Besides our coterie, which is not united by
very strong bonds, there are peasant enthu-

siasts. Antonevich organized and formed them. Rylski and Stempkovski led them for a time, but to-day these are all fools who know not what they want, they talk Little Russian and drink common vodka — that is the whole matter."

" And what other coteries are there?"

" Clearly outlined, there are no more; but there are various shades. Some are connected by a communion of scientific ideas, others by a common social standpoint. Thou wilt find here democrats, aristocrats, liberals, ultra-montanes, frolickers, women-hunters, idlers, if thou wish, and finally sunburnt laborers."

" Who passes for the strongest head?"

" Among students?"

" Yes."

" That depends on the branch. Some say that Augustinovich knows much; I will add that he does not know it well. For connected solid work and science Gustav is distinguished."

" Ah!"

" But they talk variously about him. Some cannot endure him. By living with him thou wilt estimate the man best, — for example, his relations with the widow. That is a sentimental bit of conduct: another man would not have acted as he has. Indeed, it is not easy to get on with her now."

"I have heard Gustav speak of her, but tell me once for all, what sort of woman is she?"

"She is a young person acquainted with all of us. Her history is a sad one. She fell in love with Potkanski, a jurist, and loved him perhaps madly. I do not remember those times — I remember Potkanski, however. He was a gifted fellow, very wealthy and industrious; in his day he was the idol of his comrades. How he came to know Helena, I cannot tell you; it is explained variously. This only is certain, that they loved each other to the death. She was not more than eighteen years of age. At last Potkanski determined to marry her. It is difficult to describe what his family did to prevent him, but Potkanski, an energetic man, stuck to his point, and married her despite every hindrance. Their married life lasted one year. He fell ill of typhoid on a sudden, and died leaving her on the street as it were, for his family seized all his property. A child which was living when he died, died also soon after. The widow was left alone, and had it not been for Gustav — well, she would have perished."

"What did Gustav do?"

"Gustav did wonders. With wretched means he prosecuted the Potkanskis. God knows whether he would have won the case, for that is a family of magnates, but he did this much: to avoid scandal, they engaged to pay the widow a slight life annuity."

"He acquitted himself bravely!"

"Of course he did, of course he did! Leave that to him! What energy! And remember it was during his first year at the University, without acquaintances, in a strange city, without means. And it is this way, my dear: a rich man can, a poor man must, help himself."

"But what obligation had he toward the widow?"

"He was Potkanski's friend, but that is still little; he loved her before she became Potkanski's wife, perhaps, but held aloof; now he makes no concealment."

"But she?"

"Oh, from the time of the misfortunes through which she passed the woman has fallen into utter torpor; she has become insane simply. She does not know what is happening to her, she is indifferent to everything. But beyond doubt thou wilt see her on this occasion, for she comes here every evening."

"And with what object?"

"I say that she is a maniac. The report is that she made the acquaintance of Potkanski here, so now she does not believe, it seems, that he is dead, and she goes around everywhere, as maniacs do usually. In fact, were he to rise from the dead, and not go to her straightway, she would surely find him here, nowhere else. We remind her, perhaps, of Potkanski; many students used to visit them."

"Does Gustav permit her to come here?"

"Potkanski never would have permitted her to come, but Gustav does not forbid her anything."

"How does she treat Gustav?"

"Like a table, a bench, a plate, or a ball of thread. She seems not to see him, but she does not avoid him, — she is always indifferent, apathetic. That must pain him, but it is his affair. — Ah! there she is! that woman coming in on the right."

When the widow entered, it grew somewhat silent. The appearance of that mysterious figure always produced an impression. Of stature a little more than medium, slender; she had a long face, bright blond hair, and dark eyes; her shoulders and bosom were rather slight, but she had the round plumpness of maiden forms: a forehead thrown back in a way scarcely discernible. She was pensive, and as dignified as if of marble. Her eyes, deeply set beneath her forehead, as it were in a shadow, were pencilled above with one delicate arch of brow. Those eyes were marvellous, steel-colored; they gleamed like polished metal, but that was a genuine light of steel. It was light and nothing more; under the glitter warmth and depth of thought were lacking. One might have said of those eyes, "They look, but they see not." They gave no idea of an object, they only reflected it. They were cold beyond description; we will add that their lids almost never blinked, but the pupils possessed a certain movement as if investigating, inquiring, seeking; still the movement was mechanical.

The rest of the widow's face answered to her eyes. Her mouth was pressed downward a little, as might be the case in a statue; the complexion monotonous, dull, pale, had a swarthy tinge. She was neither very charming nor very beautiful; she was accurately pretty.

This in the woman was wonderful, that though her face was torpid apparently, she had in her whole person something which attracted the masculine side of human nature inexplicably. In that lay her charm. She was statuesque to the highest degree, but to the highest degree also a woman. She attracted and also repelled. Gustav felt this best. It was difficult to reconcile with that cold torpor the impression which she produced, which seemed as it were not of her, but aside from her.

She was like a sleeping flower ; pain had so put her to sleep. In reality the blows which she had received were like strokes of an axe on the head. Let us remember that in the career of the woman brief moments of happiness were closed by two coffins. As a maiden she had loved ; he whom she had loved was no longer alive. As a wife she had given birth to a child; the child was dead. That which law had given her, which had been the cause and effect of her life, had vanished. Thenceforth she ceased to live, she only existed. Imagine a plant which is cut at the top and the root ; such was Helena. Torn from the past and debarred from the future, at first she bore within her a dim belief that a shameful injustice had been wrought on her. At the moment of her pain she threw out, it is difficult to know at whom, this question, as unfathomable as the bottomless pit:

Why has this happened? No answer came from the blue firmament, or the earth, or the fields, or the forest; the injustice remained injustice. The sun shone and the birds sang on as before. Then that unfortunate heart withdrew into itself with its own pain and became deadened.

No answer came, but her mind grew diseased — she lost belief in the death of her husband, she thought that he had taken the weeping child in his arms and gone somewhere, but that he might return any moment. Then, altogether incapable of another thought, she sought him with that bitter mechanical movement of the eyes. She went to the restaurant, thinking to find him there where she had made his acquaintance.

Unfortunately she did not die, but found a valiant arm which strove to snatch her from error, and a breast which wished to give her warmth. The effort was vain, but it saved her life. Gustav's love secured her rescue and protection, as it were by the tenure of a spider-web which did not let her go from the earth. His voice cried to her, "Stay," and though there was no echo in her, she remained, without witness of herself, indifferent, a thing, not a human being.

Such was the widow.

She entered the room and stood near the door, like a stone statue, in gloomy majesty. It was warm and smoky around her, the last sounds of a song were quivering in the air yet. A little coarse and a little dissolute was the song, and on that impure background bloomed the widow like a water-lily on a turbid pool.

Silence came. They respected her in that place. In her presence even Augustinovich became endurable. Some remembered Potkanski, others inclined their heads before her misfortune. There were also those who revered her beauty. The assembly assumed in her presence its seemliest aspect.

Gustav brought up an armchair to Pani Helena, and taking her warm shawl went to a corner to Yosef, who, attracted and astonished, turned his gleaming eyes at the widow.

Gustav began a conversation with him.

"That is she," said he, in an undertone.

"I understand."

"Do not show thyself to her much. The poor woman! every new face brings her disappointment, she is always looking for her husband."

"Art thou acquainted with her long?"

"This is the second year. I was a witness

and best man at Potkanski's wedding." Gustav smiled bitterly. "Since his death I see her daily."

"Vasilkevich says that thou hast given her aid and protection."

"I have, and I have not; some one had to attend to that, and I occupied myself with it; but such protection as mine — Do what is possible, work, fly, run — misery upon misery! so that sometimes despair seizes hold of a man."

"But the family?"

"What family?"

"His."

"They injure her!" cried Gustav, with violence.

"But they are rich, are they not?"

"Aristocrats! Hypocrites! They and I have not finished yet. They will remember long the injustice done to this dove. Listen to me, Yosef. Were a little child of that family to beg a morsel of bread of me from hunger, I would rather throw the bread to a dog."

"Oh, a romance!"

"Wrong me not, Yosef. I am poor, I waste no words. Potkanski when in the hospital regained consciousness just before death, and said, 'Gustav, to thee I leave my wife; care for her.' I answered, 'I will care for her.' 'Thou wilt not let her die of hunger?' 'I will not,' said I. 'Let no one offend her; take vengeance on any one who tries to do her an injury.' 'As God is merciful in life to me, I will avenge her,' said I. He quenched after that, like a candle. There thou hast the whole story."

"Not the whole story, not all, brother!"

"Vasilkevich told thee the rest. Very well! I will repeat the same to thee. I have no one on earth, neither father nor mother. I myself am in daily want, and she alone binds me to life." He indicated the widow with his eyes.

And here Yosef, little experienced yet, had a chance to estimate what passion is when it rises in a youthful breast and adds fire to one's blood. That dry and bent Gustav seemed to him at that moment to gain strength and vigor; he seemed to him loftier, more manly; he shook his hair as a lion shakes his mane, and on his face a flush appeared.

"Well, gentlemen," began Vasilkevich, "the hour is late, and sleep is not awaiting all of us after leaving this meeting-place. One more song, and then whoso wishes may say his good-night."

He of the maiden face who sat at the piano
struck some well-known notes, then a few
youthful voices sounded, but afterward a
whole chorus of them raised the song dear
to students, "Gaudeamus" (Let us rejoice).

Yosef went nearer the piano than others.
He stood with his side face turned to the
widow, under the light; but the lamp hanging
near the wall cast his profile in one line of
light. After a while the widow's eyes fell
on that line, connecting it unquietly with her
own thoughts. On a sudden she rose, as pale
as marble, with a feverish gleam in her eyes,
stretched forth her arms, and cried, —

"My Kazimir, I have found thee!"

In her voice were heard hope, alarm, joy,
and awakening. All were silent. Every eye
turned toward Yosef, and a quiver ran through
those who had known Potkanski. In the light
and shade that tall, strong figure seemed a
repetition of the dead man.

"I was not careful," muttered Gustav, on
his way home about daybreak. "H'm! well,
her trouble has passed, but she was excited!
He is really like him — The devils take it!
But the cursed asthma stifles me to-day."

CHAPTER II

YOSEF meditated long over the choice of his course. "I have given my clear word of honor not to waste myself in life, therefore I meditate," said he to Vasilkevich.

And here it must be confessed that the University roused him in no common manner. From various points of the world youth journeyed thither, like lines of storks. Some were entering to satisfy their mental thirst, others were going away. Some hurried in to gain knowledge as bees gather honey. They assembled, they scattered, they went in crowds, they drew from science, they drew from themselves, they drew from life. They gave animation and they received it, they spared life or they squandered it, they pressed forward, they halted, they fell, they conquered, and they were broken with their lives. Bathing in that sea, some of them were drowned, others swam to shore. Movement, uproar, activity dominated immensely.

The University was like a general ovarium where brains were to be propagated. It opened every year, giving forth ripe fruits, and taking in straightway new nurslings. Men were born there a second time. It was beautiful to see how youth, like waves of water, rolled forth to the world yearly, bearing light to the ignorant, as it were provisions to the human field. To such a sea the boat of life brought Yosef. Where was he to attach himself? Various courses of study, like harbors, enticed him. Whither was he to turn? He meditated long; at last he sailed in.

He chose the medical course.

"Happen what may, I must be rich," said he, deciding the question of choice.

But this decision was only because Yosef, with his open mind, had immense regard for the secrets of science. Both literature and law attracted him, but natural sciences he looked on as the triumph of human thought. He had brought even from school this opinion of those sciences. In his school there had been a young teacher of chemistry, a great enthusiast, who, placing his hand on his heart, spoke thus one day to those of his pupils who were finishing their course, —

"Believe me, my boys, except natural science there is nothing but guesswork."

It is true that the prefect of the school while

closing religious exercises, affirmed that only
the science of the Church can bring man to
everlasting happiness. At this Yosef, whom
the prefect had already called a "vile heretic,"
made such an ugly grimace that he roused
the laughter of all who were present, but he
drew down on his own head thunders partly
deserved.

So he chose the medical course.

Vasilkevich influenced him in this regard.
Vasilkevich, a student himself, had, rightly or
wrongly, an immense influence on his comrades. It happened that at a students' talk
a certain grammarian, a philologist, showed
with less truth than hypocrisy that a man
given to science should devote himself to it
exclusively, forget the world, forget happiness, and incarnate himself in science, — be
simply its expression, its basis, its word. In
this deduction there was more of false enthusiasm and stiltedness than sincerity. "People
tell us," continued the speaker, "that an Ice-
landic fisherman, who had forgotten himself in
gazing at the aurora borealis, did not guard
against currents. The waters bore him away
to deep places, and he, with eyes fixed on
those northern lights, became entirely ruddy
in their gleams, till at last the spirit of the

abyss bore him away and confined him under the glassy wave, but in the fisherman's eyes the lights remained pictured.

"There is science and life!" added he. "The man who has once inclined his forehead before science may let the waves of life bear him to any depth, the light will remain with him."

There are principles in the world which one does not recognize, but to come out against them a man needs no small share of courage. So among students one and another were silent, but Vasilkevich panted angrily and rose from his seat; at last he burst out, —

"Tfu! empty words! Let a German consort himself in that way with science, not us! In my mind science is for men, not men for science. Let the German turn himself into a parchment. Thy fisherman was a fool. If he had worked with his oar, he might have seen the lights and brought fish to his children. But again look at the question in this way: Poor people suffer and perish from hunger and cold, and wilt thou tear thyself free of the world and be for men a burden instead of an assistance?

"Oi, Tetvin, Tetvin!" This was the name of the previous speaker. "Consider the sense,

not the sound of thy words. Thou art able
to unite folly with reason! To-day it seems
to thee that thou wilt predict luck from a
few faded cards. Not true! When the moment comes and thy breast aches about the
heart, thou wilt yearn honestly for happiness
in love. For example, in Lithuania, I have
a pair of old people in a cottage, my father
and mother, as white as doves, and one of
them says to the other things of me which
are beyond my merits, things which might be
told of a golden king's son. What would
my worth be were I to shut myself up in a
book, not think of them, and neglect them in
their old age? None whatever. — Well, I
come here and I forget neither science nor
them nor myself. And I am not alone.
Every man who tills a field has the right to
eat bread from it. That to begin with! Science is science; let not a scholar tear himself
loose from life, let him not be an incompe-
tent. A scholar is a scholar; but if he cannot button his shirt, if he does not support
his own children, and has no care for his
wife? Why not reconcile the practice of
life with science? Why not bring science
into one's career and enliven science itself
with life?"

Thus spoke Vasilkevich. He spoke and panted with excitement.

The point is not in this whether he spoke truth or falsehood; we have repeated the conversation because Yosef, by nature inclined to be practical, took it to heart; he considered, meditated, thought, and chose the medical course.

Happen what may, a man brings to the world certain tendencies.

Yosef's mind was realistic by nature, in some way he clung rather to things than ideas — he had therefore no love for dialectics of any sort. He preferred greatly to see an object as it was, and had no wish to have it seem better than it was. The movement of mind in men's heads is of two sorts: one starts eternally from the centre of existence, the other refers each object to some other. Men of the first kind enter into things already investigated, and give them life by connecting them with the main source of existence by a very slender thread of knowledge. The first are the so-called creative capacities; the second grasp things in some fashion, compare them, classify them, and understand them only through arranging and bringing them into classes, — those are the scientific capacities. The first men

are born to create, the second to investigate.
The difference between them is like that between a spendthrift and a miser, between
exhaling and inhaling. It is difficult to tell
which is the better: the first have the gift
of creating; the second of developing, and
above all of digesting. In the second this
is active; true, the stomach has that power
also. A perfect balance between these powers
constitutes genius. In such a case there is a
natural need of broad movements.

Yosef had the second capacity, the classify-
ing. He not only had it, but he knew that he
had it; this conviction preserved him in life
from many mistakes, and gave a certain balance
to his wishes and capacities. He never under-
took a thing that for him was impossible. He
calculated with himself. And, finally, he had
much enthusiasm, which in his case might have
been called persistence in science. Having
a mind which was fond of examining everything soberly, he wanted to see everything
well; but to see well one must know thoroughly. He was unable to guess, he wished
to know.

This was why he never learned anything
half-way. As a spider surrounds a fly, he surrounded his subject of investigation diligently

with a network of thought, he drew it into himself; it might be said that he sucked it out of the place where it was and finally digested it. His thoughts had also a high degree of activity. He desired, a natural attribute of youth. He was free of conceit. Frequently he rejected an opinion accepted by all, specially for this reason, that it had importance behind it. It must be confessed, however, that in this case he endeavored to find everything that was against it; when he did not find enough, he yielded. He had, besides, no little energy in thinking and doing.

All this composed his strength, his weapon, partly acquired, partly natural. We forgot to say that he had in addition two thousand rubles.

When he had estimated these supplies, he betook himself to medicine. But the greater the enthusiasm with which he betook himself to his specialty the more was he disenchanted at first. He wanted to know, but now only memory was required. In that case any man might succeed; at least it was a question of memory and will, not of reason. One needed a memory of the eyes, a memory of the hands; one had to put into the head seriously the first and second and tenth, from time to time like grain into a storehouse. That was well-nigh the work of a handicraftsman; the mental organism gained no profit from these supplies, for it did not digest nor work them over. Nutrition was lacking there. The philosophy of the physical structure of organisms may be compared in subtlety and in immensity of result with all others; but Yosef was only beginning to become acquainted with the organism itself; indications as to whether there existed any philosophy of those sciences were not given him thus far.

But having once begun he had to wade farther. He waded. But the technical side of scientific labor was disagreeable, thankless, full of hidden difficulties and unexpected secrets, frequently obscure, often barely visible, most frequently repelling, always costing labor. One might have said that nature had declared war against the human mind at this stage. Yosef struggled with these moral difficulties, but he advanced. That technic had a gloomy side also in his eye: it had an evil effect morally.

It disclosed the end of life without indicating whether a continuation existed. The veil was removed from death without the least hesitation. All the deformity of that sub-

terranean toiler was exhibited with uncon-
cealed insolence. That which remained of
the dead was also a cynical promise to the
living. Death appeared to say in open daylight, "Till we meet in the darkness!" This
seemed an announcement bearing terrible
proofs of the helplessness of man before an
implacable, malicious, loathsome, and shame-
less power. This power when seen face to
face, roused in young minds a violent reaction, — a reaction expressed in the following manner: "Let us lose no time, let us
make use of life, for sooner or later the
devils will take everything!"

In such occupations delicacy of feeling
was dimmed by degrees; indifference was de-
graded to coarseness, ambition to envy, love
passed into passion, passion into impulse.
Love was like the sun seen through a smoked
glass; one felt the heat, but saw not the
radiance.

Yosef warded off these impressions; he
shook himself free of them, he cast them
away, and went forward.

Finally, he had to be true to his principle.
He who has confidence in one career has not
in another; that which he has chosen seems
best to him. In that which Yosef had chosen

everything from the time of Hippocrates downward reposed on experience. Seeing, hearing, tasting, smelling, and feeling are the only criteria on which the whole immense structure stands even in our day.

So men believe, especially young men, as the most different in everything from their elders. All that has come to science by ways aside from experience, is doubtful. Each man judges according to his own thought the ideas of others. The hypothesis of anything existing outside of experience, even if true, seems through such a glass frivolous. "Only investigated things have existence. The connection between cause and effect is a necessity of thought, but only in man. History is a chronicle more or less scandalous; law rests on experience of modes of living in society, speculation is a disease of the mind."

Yosef did not ward off these thoughts, since they did not hinder him in advancing.

As to the rest he worked on.

CHAPTER III

A MONTH passed.

The evening was fair, autumnal; the sun was quenching slowly on the towers of Kieff and on the distant grave-mounds of the steppe. Its light was still visible on the roof above Yosef and Gustav. Both were bent over their work and, sitting in silence, used the last rays of evening with eagerness. Gustav had returned from the city not long before; he was suffering and pale, he panted more than usual. On his face a certain uneasiness was manifest, vexation, even pain; this he strove to conceal, but still it was evident from the fever of his eyes. Both men were silent. It was clear, however, that Gustav wished to break the silence, for he turned to Yosef frequently; but since it seemed as though the first word could be spoken only with difficulty, he sank back to his book again. At last evident impatience was expressed on his face; he seized his cap from the table, and rose.

" What o'clock is it now ? " asked he.

" Six."

" Why art thou not going to the widow's ? Thou goest every day to visit her."

Yosef turned toward Gustav, —

" It was at her request that I went with thee to her lodgings the first time. Let us not mention the subject. I do not care to speak of that which would be disagreeable to both of us; for that matter, we understand each other perfectly. I will not see the widow to-day, or to-morrow, or any day. Thou hast my word and hand on that."

They stood then in silence, Yosef with extended hand. Gustav, hesitating and disturbed by the awkward position, finally pressed the palm of his comrade.

Evidently words came to both with difficulty; one did not wish to use heartfelt expressions, the other heartfelt thanks. After a while they parted.

Men's feelings are strange sometimes, and the opposite of those which would seem the reward of noble deeds. Yosef promised Gustav not to see Pani Helena, the widow. Whether he loved her or not, that was a sacrifice on his part, for in his toilsome and monotonous existence she was the only bright point around which his thought loved to circle. Though thinking about her was only the occupation of moments snatched from hard labor and devoted to rest and mental freedom, to renounce such moments was to deprive rest of its charm, it was to remove a motive from life at a place where feeling might bud out and blossom.

Yosef, after thinking a little, did this without hesitation. He made a sacrifice.

Still, when Gustav had gone from the room, there was on Yosef's face an expression of distaste, even anger. Was that regret for the past, or for the deed done a moment before?

No.

When he extended his hand to Gustav, the latter hesitated in taking it. Not to accept a sacrifice given by an energetic soul is to cover the deed of sacrifice itself with a shadow of ridicule; and this in the mind of him who makes the sacrifice is to be ungrateful, and to cast a grain of deep hatred into the rich field of vanity.

But to accept a rival's sacrifice is for a soul rich in pride to place one's own " I " under the feet of some other man morally; it is to receive small coppers of alms thrust hastily into a hand which had not been stretched forth for anything.

Pride prefers to be a creditor rather than a debtor.

Therefore Gustav when on the street twisted his mouth in bitter irony, and muttered through his pressed lips.

Better and better. Favor, favor! Bow down now to Pan Yosef daily, and thank him. A pleasant life for thee, Gustav!

And he fell into bitter, deep meditation. He ceased even to think of himself, he was merely dreaming painfully. He felt a kind of gloomy echo in his soul, while striving to summon up the remembrance of even one happy moment. That echo sounded in him like a broken chord. The mind and soul in the man were divided. One tortured half cried hurriedly for rest; the other half, energetic and gloomy, strove toward life yet. One half of his mind saw light and an object; the other turned moodily toward night and nothingness. To finish all, there was something besides in this sorrowing man which made sport of its own suffering; something like a malicious demon which with one hand indicated his own figure to him, pale, ugly, bent, and pointed out with the other, as it were in the clouds in the brightness of morning, Helena Potkanski, in marble repose, in splendid beauty.

Torn apart with the tumult of this internal battle, he went forward alone, almost without knowing whither. Suddenly he heard behind a well-known voice singing in bass the glad song: —

> "Hop! hop! hop! hop!
> And the horseshoe firmly fastened."

He looked around — it was Vasilkevich and Augustinovich.

"Whither art thou hastening, Gustav?" asked the first.

"I? Ha! whither — " He looked at his watch. "It is too early to visit Pani Helena. I am going at present to the club."

"Well, go straight to the widow."

"What? Why?"

"Woe!" exclaimed Augustinovich, raising his hand toward heaven; and without noticing passers-by, he fell to declaiming loudly: —

> "The castle where joyousness sounded
> Is shrouded in mourning to-day;
> On its wall the wild weeds are growing,
> At its gate the faithful dog howls."

"Thou hast no reason to visit the club," added Vasilkevich.

"What has happened?"

"Gloom is there now incubating a tempest," replied Augustinovich.

" But say what has happened."

" Misfortune."

" Of what sort? "

" Ghastly ! "

" Vasilkevich, speak in human fashion ! "

" The University government has closed our club.   Some one declared that students assemble there."

" When did this happen? "

" Two hours since."

" We must go there and learn on the spot."

" I do not advise thee to do so.   They will put thee in prison."

" They will bind thy white palms with a rope — "

" Augustinovich, be quiet!   Why did they not do this in the evening?   They might have caught us all like fish in a net."

" Well, they cared more for closing the club than for seizing us;   but were a man to go now, beyond doubt they would seize him."

" But whither are ye going? "

" We are going with a watchword of alarm; the clans send a fiery cross — "

" Speak low, I beg thee! "

" Yes, valiant Roderic."

" True, true," interrupted Vasilkevich; " we

are on the way to warn others, so farewell, or go with us."

"I cannot."

"Where wilt thou go?"

"To Pani Helena's."

"Farewell."

"Till we meet again!"

When he was alone, Gustav rubbed his hands, a smile of satisfaction lighted up his gloomy face for a moment. He was pleased with the closing of the club, for he ceased to fear that Helena, on learning of Yosef's decision, might wish to visit the club to see him there. His fears were well founded. Gustav remembered that despite prayers and arguments he had barely, by the promise of bringing Yosef to her lodgings, been able to restrain her from this improper step. Now he had no cause for fear.

After a while he pulled the bell at the widow's dwelling.

"How is thy mistress?" asked he of the servant girl.

"She is well, but walking in the room and talking to herself."

Gustav entered.

Pani Helena's dwelling was composed of two narrow chambers, with windows looking out

on a garden; the first chamber was a small
drawing-room, the second she used as a bed-
chamber, which Gustav now entered. The
upper part of the window in the bed-chamber
was divided by a narrow strip of wood from
the lower part, and had colored panes arranged
in the form of a flower, blue and red alternately.
In one corner stood a small mahogany table
covered with a soft velvet spread. On the table
stood two portraits; one in an inlaid wooden
frame represented a young man with a high
forehead, blond hair, and handsome aristocratic features, — that was Potkanski; the other
was Pani Helena. On her knees was her little
daughter dressed in white. Before the portraits lay a garland of immortelles entwined
with crape and with a sprig of dry myrtle.

At the opposite end of the room, between
two beds divided by a narrow space, was a
small cradle, now empty, once filled with the
twittering and noise of an infant. Its cover,
colored green by the light of the panes, seemed
to move slightly. One might have thought
that a little hand would be thrust out any moment, and a joyous head look at its mother.

Silent sadness was in the atmosphere of the
place. The leaves of the acacia which looked
in through the window were outlined darkly on

the floor, and, moved by the wind, yielded to the quivering light and returned again. Near the door was a small statuette, representing the angel of baptism with hands extended as if to bless; at its feet was a holy-water pot.

At the moment of which we are speaking the head of the angel was bright in colored gleams, as if with a mild glory of sweetness, of repose and innocence. There was, moreover, great silence in the chamber. The sorrow of that day equalled former gladness. What delight and prattling when Potkanski, returning in the evening tired with toil, embraced his wife with one arm, and putting back her golden hair, kissed her forehead, which at that time was calm and serene. How much quiet, deep joy when they stood in silence breast to breast and eye to eye, like statues of Love! Afterward they ran to the cradle where the little one, twittering with itself in various ways, and raising its tiny feet, laughed at the happy parents.

Now the cradle was empty. Marvellously affecting was that cradle. It seemed that the child was there.

More than once, in the first period of her misfortune, the widow, when she woke in the night, put her hand carefully into the cradle with the conviction that God must have pitied her, and, removing the child from the coffin, placed it back in the cradle.

In a word, those walls had seen much joy, lulled by the happiness of serene love, then tears as large as pearls, then despair, which was silent, deathlike, and finally stubborn, mad.

Such was the sleeping-room of that widow, and such were the thoughts which were roused at sight of the apartment. The little drawing-room, like all of its kind, had a sort of slight elegance and much emptiness. In that chamber, too, the echoes of past moments seemed to wander. It was well lighted, clean, but common; the room of the servant adjoined it, — a small dark closet with an entrance on the stairway and a wooden partition.

Such was the former residence of Potkanski. After his death it was difficult to understand whence the means came to keep up such lodgings; this, however, pertained to Gustav, he knew what he was doing. There were no claims on the part of the owner; how this was managed we shall explain somewhat later.

As often as Gustav entered that dwelling he trembled.

In a place which was full of her presence, where everything that was not she was for

4

her, he felt always a kind of weight on his breast, as if some hand were pressing his heart down more deeply. But that pressure was for him delightful. It was a contraction of his breast as if to inhale more air. To be pressed down by a feeling of happiness is almost to be happy, except that beyond it lies an immense shoreless space of desires. It inundates the whole man then, enters into his blood, manifests itself in the trembling of his words, in the glitter of his eyes. That desire itself does not know what it wants. Between too little and too much there is no boundary in the present case. This is the bashful desire of everything. A man is more daring externally than internally; his own words frighten him; it seems to him that some one else is saying something, he guards his own glances, he wants to laugh spasmodically or to burst out sobbing. He loves, he honors, he makes an angel of a woman, and then desires that same angel as a woman.

Gustav experienced this when he entered the widow's apartments. Every kind of desire which spirit and blood joined together can summon, flew to him from all sides, like flocks of winged creatures.

She stood before him. She was pale; on

her lips appeared a slight trace of ruddiness.
Her delicate profile was outlined on the background of the window like a silhouette. She
held a comb in her hand, and, standing before
the small silver-framed mirror, was combing
her hair. Luxuriant tresses wound like waves
around her pale forehead. That golden mass
flowed down over her shoulders and breast,
and seemed to drop like amber.

Seeing Gustav, she greeted him with her
hand and with a barely perceptible smile.

The widow had emerged from her former
lethargy. That sudden and violent shock which
the sight of Yosef at the restaurant had called
forth roused her, enlivened her. She began to
think. One thing alone was she unable at first
to explain. Yosef's form was so confounded
in her mind with that of Potkanski that she
did not know herself which was her former
husband. That was the remnant of her in-
sanity. But soon a ray of light returned to
that beclouded mind. She begged Gustav to
let her see Yosef. Gustav, though unwilling,
agreed to this. With yearning did she wait
for the evening when she was to look at that
reminder of her former happiness. Not Yosef
was she seeking, but the reminder; hence he
was for her an absolute necessity.

Then gradually and quite imperceptibly the past changed into the present, the dream into a reality. Yosef, noting this, had promised Gustav not to visit her; to prepare Helena and announce this news to her pertained to Gustav.

It was easy to foresee the impression which this would make. She clasped her hands and threw back her head. A torrent of hair covered her shoulders with a rustle.

"Where shall I see him?" asked she, insistently.

Gustav was silent.

"I must see him here or elsewhere. He is so like Kazimir— My God, I live entirely by that memory, Pan Gustav."

Gustav was silent. He was made almost indignant by that blind egotism of Pani Helena. The drama began to play in him again. She begged him to do everything to undermine his own happiness. No! to act thus he would have to be a fool. But on the other hand— it was Helena who made the prayer. He bit his lips till the blood came, and was silent. Moreover, something belongs to him even from life. Everything that in him made up the man opposed her prayers with desperate energy. Meanwhile she continued to urge,—

"Pan Gustav, you will arrange so that I shall see him? I wish to see him. Why do you do me such an injustice?"

Cold sweat covered Gustav's forehead; he stretched his hands to his face, and in a gloomy voice answered, —

"I do you no injustice, but " — here his voice quivered, he made an effort not to fall at her feet and cry out, "But I love thee, do not torture me!" — "he does not wish to come here," concluded he, almost inaudibly.

He would have given much to avoid this moment. Helena covered her face with her hands and dropped into the armchair. Silence continued for a while, and the rustling of leaves was heard outside the window; inside the soul of a man was writhing in a conflict with itself. To bring Yosef, to take Helena from him, was for Gustav to unbridle misfortune.

The struggle was brief; he knelt before Helena, and putting his lips to her hand, said in a broken voice, —

"I shall do what I can. He will come here. What am I to any one? He will come, but I cannot tell when — I will bring him myself."

Soon after, in leaving the widow's lodgings, he muttered through his set teeth, —

"Yes, he will come; but it is not I who will

bring him — he will come in a month — in two months — perhaps I shall be at rest."

An attack of coughing interrupted further meditation. Gustav wandered through the streets for a long time; when he returned home, it struck two in the church belfry.

Yosef was sleeping; he was breathing uniformly, quietly; the light of the lamp fell on his high forehead and open breast. Gustav looked feverishly at that breast. His eyes gleamed with hatred. He sat thus about an hour. All at once he trembled, he came to himself. A sensation was roused in him entirely opposite to any which he had felt up to that moment, a sensation of hunger; he went to the book-shelves, and taking a piece of brown bread, fell to eating it hastily.

CHAPTER IV

AUTUMN was approaching. It was cold in the rooms of the poorer students. Wrapped in their blankets and wearing caps, they warmed themselves with study. The rooms of those who had something with which to heat their stoves were swarming with comrades. No one visited the club any longer. At first there were efforts to select some other place for a club, but it ended in nothing, because Gustav on the one hand, and on the other Yosef, who had acquired considerable influence among students, resisted together; more especially Yosef, who held that clubs consumed too much time and were of small utility. He desired to introduce reform in this regard, and at last he succeeded. In spite of all opposing opinions he combated for that idea in the University, and especially at Vasilkevich's rooms, where students met with more willingness than elsewhere.

Vasilkevich roomed with Karvovski, or rather the latter with Vasilkevich, for though Karvovski was very wealthy (he was that pale youth who had played on the piano to his comrades in the club) and paid by far the greater part of the rent for their lodgings, the soul and the pivot of this male housekeeping was our Lithuanian.

The friendship between these two young men deserved admiration and even envy. One, delicate, pampered, beautiful, with a head full of the loftiest dreams, mild-mannered and be-loved of all, slipped lightly through life in comfort and plenty. The other, a genuine Lithuanian, ugly in appearance, pock-marked, with closely cut hair and flashing eyes, viva-cious, laborious, energetic, and profoundly in-structed, was for the first as a guardian or elder brother.

Vasilkevich possessed a warm heart, and was made, as the phrase runs, for the palm of the hand. Once when Karvovski fell danger-ously ill, he nursed him night and day with real unparalleled self-denial, and when at last he recovered, the Lithuanian wept and scolded him from delight. " Oh, thou jester," said he, " what a trick for thee to fall ill; but just try it a second time ! "

The students called them a chosen pair, and an old blind grandfather (minstrel) of the Ukraine who begged not far from their lodgings and to whom they gave frequent alms, spoke of them as the "kind-hearted young lords."

Many circumstances united them, but especially one which we shall mention immediately. They spent a summer vacation in the country at Karvovski's. Karvovski had a sister, weakly and not comely, but with wonderful kindness of heart, quiet, calm, a genuine angel, with a sunburnt little face and a fragile figure. That young maiden was loved by Vasilkevich; he loved her in his own way, very deeply, with faith in her and in his love, and, what is more, she loved him. Her parents did not know much of the matter, or if they did know they had no wish to hinder the young people. The maiden was ill-favored, he was honest and reliable; these facts balanced the small inequality of social position. Moreover, they did not wish to deprive their son of a society which in every regard could be only of use to him.

This Lithuanian had another good side; he loved his parents beyond everything, — the "old people," as he called them. These old people lived in remotest Jmud, near Livonia; they were poor, their son helped them. His father was a forester. The old man had a small home in the wilderness: round about him the forest sounded and the wave plashed; beyond the forest and the wave were other forests and other waves, — a remote corner it was behind the lakes. The devil lived there, according to local traditions, but somehow that devil did not trouble the old people. Such was the place in which Vasilkevich first saw the light of day.

When as a boy he went fishing, he met ducks beyond the lake, he found nests in the swamps. He was of a healthy and active disposition. Nature had cradled him; he was taught by birds, water, and trees. From the fern of the forest to the birch which knew not where in the heavens to put its head, all was for him a book the first words of which he himself learned to read. The birds of the Commonwealth explained their laws to him; once he saw how beavers made dams with their tails in the rivers; he knew that by following the voice of the bee-eater he could find hidden bee-nests; he knew how to take their young from the badgers. He even brought home young wolves to the house with him.

When he had grown up sufficiently, his father taught him to read; the old man drew out of a box some rusty coins, and sent the boy to school; then difficult times set in. There was need to learn: so he learned. It

would be a long tale to tell how much and
what he passed through before he reached the
University and began to be the man whom
we know at present.

His parents returned his love a hundred-fold.
In truth, they were a pair of doves whitened
by age, loving each other, in agreement and
happiness.

Happiness and peace dwelt in that cottage.
Such bright spots on the earth are met with,
though rarely, like oases in a desert. The old
people enjoyed each other, and went side by
side as in the first days after marriage; they
called each other falcon and berry. What joy
there was when that son came home for vacation, no tongue can tell, no pen can describe.
With Vasilkevich came Karvovski. The old
people loved and petted him also, but he was
not for them as their Yasek, whom they simply
called " Ours."

Often when the young men were tired from
racing a whole day through the wilderness,
the old people after going to bed talked
in a low voice about them. This is what
Karvovski heard once through their chamber
partition, —

" He is a handsome boy, that Karvovski,"
said the old man.

"But ours is handsomer," answered the old woman.

"Oh, handsomer, handsomer!"

Meanwhile that "Ours" was what is called ugly, but through the prism of parental love he seemed the most beautiful on earth. It is not reality itself, but the heart with which we approach it that gives things their form and color.

But let us return to Kieff and to our acquaintances.

It is nothing wonderful that with such hosts as Vasilkevich and Karvovski their dwelling, in which among other things stood a perfect stove, became a centre for many students. Even the intelligence of the University assembled there; literary evenings were established. All who felt a vein for letters made public their productions in those rooms. The long autumn evenings were turned into genuine literary sessions. It would be difficult to enumerate the burning thoughts which were uttered there by youthful lips.

Vasilkevich, Karvovski, Yosef, in a little while Gustav, and especially Augustinovich, took the lead in those meetings. Yosef tried his creative powers, but somehow he did not succeed, he had not the talent, simply; he did

not know how to fashion, how to create, how to
attach his own ideas to that golden thread of
fantasy which bathes all things in rainbow
tints before it gives them to the world warmed
and illuminated, or bright as a summer night's
lightning.

But in recompense he had another kind of
power. He judged soundly, and what is more,
with keenness. After he had read a produc-
tion of his own he analyzed it in presence of
all; joyous laughter continued till late in the
apartments. In like manner did he treat the
productions of others; if he ridiculed the
chips flew from those first offerings placed on
the altar of art. He was able so to arrange
his voice and expression of face to the current of his words that when he wished the
gloomiest subject roused the most laughter.
This obtained for him great consideration.
Those who, feeling a sympathy for the moon,
struck the sentimental chords of their hearts,
dreaded him as they might have dreaded Satan.

Vasilkevich described his Lithuanian lakes
and forests pithily. From time to time Karvovski permitted himself lyric verses in which dew,
tears, lilies of the valley, and sighs spoke with
each other in the manner of people. In this
case it was not a question of judgment, but of

the love of a village shepherd for a birch of the field which after his death "took up and withered," according to the words of those pathetic verses.

There were better and worse things in that assembly; humor appeared often, but at times something superior which was worth listening to, especially since by degrees through exercise and criticism capacities of greater or less power were manifested.

But Augustinovich towered above every one at all times. It happened more than once, God forgive, that he came drunk to the meeting, his manuscript crushed, soiled, and written fragmentarily on anything; but when he began to read all else was forgotten, the soul clung to his words. More than one student used hands and head, drew out of himself all that was best, wrote a thing that was more or less good, but common. "That lurking soul" caught up a pen right there in the room amid noise and conversation, but sheets and sheets flew from his hand and dropped under the table. When he had finished writing he picked up the sheets, arranged them, and sat down with indifference; but all listened, and more than one man envied him secretly. His figures were as if living, so complete were they; under

the wave of his words thought flowed in a
hundred colors, like a serpent glittering with
jewels. When he spoke of love you felt the
beating of a beloved heart on your own; when
he rose with the strength of enthusiasm, the
thunder of words roared, and the mind dazzled
by lightning flashes quivered in fear; when
in the low fall of words he depicted some feeling touchingly, the odor of roses and myrtle
was discovered in the air, the fern blossomed
in the moonlight, from some place beyond the
forest and the pine wood, the song of a maiden
floated out on the dew.

Ah, he was gifted! Beautiful words and
beautiful thoughts fell from him of themselves,
not having apparent connection with the man.
Those were blossoms on a quagmire. Revela-
tions of humor, in which moral fall accompanied
cynicism, testified best of all to this.

"Ei, Augustinovich! Augustinovich!" said
the students to him then, "with thy gifts, were
there not such a devil in thee, what couldst
thou not do, O thou scapegrace!"

"For this very reason I wish to drown him.
Have ye not something here to drink?" replied he.

Gustav had been present at those meetings
a few times; but he did not like Karvovski.

simply because all liked him. The more difficult his career was, the more clouds obscured
the horizon of his love, the more irritable and
embittered did he become. Passionate and
unsuccessful attachments have this peculiarity,
that they develop hatreds just as passionate.
Such a hatred not directed to any person or
thing yet had occupied Gustav's breast and was
resting like rust in it. He hated all who had
what he lacked. He felt as if wronged, and
for every wrong such natures are accustomed
to pay, even though they pay only in theory.

He withdrew, therefore, from the society of
students, though among them alone existed
hearts which could beat for him. He knew
this, and in spite of his hatred for all men he
loved students; still he shut himself up within
his own bosom. Sympathy humiliated him.
He suspected the existence of pity in all
places, and was afraid of it.

Finally, they learned this, that Yosef had
promised him not to visit Helena. This information had not come from Yosef, but from
Gustav himself; he had told it in a moment of
irritation. Naturally this raised Yosef in the
opinion of his comrades. Gustav was angry.
Between him and Yosef a dark cloud of dislike had intervened.

The widow spoke to him of Yosef with greater and greater insistence, with increasing force, with rising passion. A process of ill-omen for Gustav, as Gustav himself thought, took place in her. The deceased Potkanski became more and more incarnate in Yosef; in this new figure Potkanski was dissolved and lost. By degrees, and just through long separation, the enthusiastic heart of Helena remembered Yosef more and more, but now for the sake of himself.

A new epoch of resuscitated happiness for the widow, of dying hope for Gustav, emerged gradually, urged on by the rude hand of necessity, — an epoch born of tears, chance, and pain.

"I may not, I may not be long in peace!" thought he. "But happen what may, I will not bring him here a second time."

Every one will divine easily what was hidden under a reflection of that sort. Gustav judged that he would be able to stifle himself by work, — he was more and more wearied; happy moments he had only in sleep.

Once he dreamed that he was at Helena's knees and kissing her hands; he felt distinctly her dear palms on his heart. Then in the dream excitement of passion he found her lips

5

with his lips, and almost suffered from excess of delight.

After that came awakening.

He saw her daily, — he was so near to her and always so distant.

He grew thinner and more emaciated; in his eyes shone feverish gleams of unbending will. That fever exhausted him, but kept him on his feet.

" I am curious to know what will come of this," muttered he through his parched lips.

But there was one side almost sublime in this gloomy exertion of suffering. Gustav was not dreaming. He took life as it was, not as it might be. In spite of the sad condition of his health, he knew how to work, and worked more than ever. To come from Pani Helena and sit down to toil needed no common strength, — such victories he won over his own nature daily. He gathered about him a number of the most capable men, and as it were to compare them with the assemblies at Vasilkevich's, he organized a circle laboring only scientifically. He and two fellow-students were writing a grammar of the Lettish languages; in spite of continual disputes with his co-workers, he stood at the head of this labor, and what he stole from suffering he gave to it.

CHAPTER V

NOTHING could be more irritating than the relations of these students.

They lived together.

At last Gustav on returning one day from Pani Helena's found Yosef's effects packed. Yosef himself was occupied in arranging his books and linen.

Both were silent till all was ready; then Yosef said, —

" Gustav, farewell! I am moving out."

Gustav reached out his hand without saying a word. They parted coldly.

On the road Vasilkevich met Yosef.

"Ho! What is this?" inquired he. "Art thou moving?"

"Thou knowest my relations with Gustav, judge thyself if I can live with him longer."

"But this is clear, it was not well for thee to leave him in his present condition of health."

" I understand, but I assure thee that I can only irritate him. Thou knowest what I have done for Gustav; he has no real reason to dislike me; but still—"

Vasilkevich pressed his hand.

Yosef's new lodgings were in a house of several stories. They consisted of two large and good-looking rooms. Besides the money which he had brought from home, Yosef immediately after his arrival found means which permitted him to save his capital to the utmost. He began to think then of a more comfortable mode of life, and at last arranged things far better really than at the beginning. From the first glance one might note ease and plenty in the new dwelling. The bed was made in good order every day, the floor swept, and in the small porcelain stove a cheerful fire burned daily, toward evening—it was so comfortable there that the soul rejoiced!

For that matter, the whole house was far better arranged than the other, it was even elegant. On the first story lived some general with his wife and two daughters, as ugly as two winter nights; on the second story lived Yosef, and a French engineer from whom the rooms were hired; and on the third some reduced count, a man immensely rich on a time, perhaps, but at that moment bankrupt; he lived in three or four rooms with his grown-up daughter and two or three servant-maids from the Ukraine. Such were Yosef's neighbors.

Soon they gave evidence of themselves, for all day in the engineer's rooms groaned a piano at which children were learning to play all the contra-dances ever danced up to that time in any land; at the general's were continual amusements, dances, and evening parties. Whole nights through there was stamping there, as in a mill, servants moving about on the stairway; there was no lack of noise and rattle.

The count alone lived quietly. There is nothing wonderful in this, that he and his daughter sat there meditating sadly over their own ruin like Jews over the ruins of Jerusalem. Yosef of course did not know them yet, but at times about dusk, by the clatter on the stairs and the heavy tread, he divined that the old count was taking his daughter to walk; but not being fond of titles or coronets, he had in truth no curiosity to look at them.

Once, however, he saw something which interested him more. A certain day, while going to his room, he saw between the first story and the second a certain bust bent over the banisters with a head altogether shapely, blue eyes, and dark hair. Those eyes, shaded by a hand, were looking carefully for something in the half light of the passage. Seeing Yosef, the head pushed forward, and with it the body, and when the student hurried on, wishing to see the young lady more nearly, he saw only two small feet in black boots and white stockings. The feet were fleeing upstairs with all speed.

"Ah, that is the countess then!" thought he.

The countess roused his curiosity. He did not know himself why in the dusk sitting in front of the fire he saw definitely before him that pair of eyes covered with the hand, the white forehead surrounded with curls of dark hair, and the feet in black boots.

A couple of evenings later when at an advanced hour he had put out the light and lain down in bed, he heard some voice singing a melancholy song in Italian. The passage and Yosef's room also were filled with those tones, youthful, resonant, sympathetic; the fond and passionate adjurations and reproaches were given out with a marvellous charm; in the stillness of night the words came forth clearly.

"Ah! the countess is singing!" murmured Yosef.

Next morning early, he knew not why, while dressing and rubbing his hands with soap stubbornly, he sang with much pathos, as if to lend himself energy.

But soon he ceased; the widow came to his mind instead of the countess. "That woman either loves me already, or she would love me very soon," thought he. He wished the return of those moments during which he had looked into her eyes. "What a strange woman!" thought he. "How that Potkanski must have loved her — ha! and Gustav!" He frowned. "If I go there, will he not grieve to death, will he not poison himself? That love will ruin him — h'm! Each answers for himself. But I am curious to know what she says since I do not visit her."

Thenceforth that moment recurred to his mind frequently when she, so pale and with outstretched arms, exclaimed, "I have found thee, my Kazimir!"

If only he wished, he could go to her, love her, and be loved by her.

This plan of probable love did not let him sleep. Like every young man, he felt the need of love; his heart beat violently, as if it wanted to burst, broken by its own strength. And so far he knew no woman except the widow. The

black boots and white stockings of the countess passed before his eyes, but that slight
imagining vanished into nothingness.

He remembered meanwhile how on a certain
time during conversation he had held the
widow's hand; he remembered what a wish he
had had to kiss it, but he remembered also how
ominously Gustav's eyes were glittering at that
moment. Jealousy seized him. Occasionally a
scarcely visible cloud, regret for a premature
promise, sped past in his soul and hid somewhere in its darkest caves. Then he repeated
in a very tragic tone, " I have promised, I will
not go."

One thing more angered him, — to people
respected and more advanced in life this would
seem a paradox, — the quiet of life angered him.
Science came to him easily, he did not expend
all his powers, and this roused distaste in him.
Fresh, active natures, like young soldiers, feel
a need of bathing in the fire of battle. This
desire of his to fight which at a more advanced
age seems to us improbable, becomes in certain
years, and quite seriously, one of the needs of
the spirit. Let us remember Yosef's monologue in Gustav's room, the first day of his coming to Kieff. He wanted then to throw down
the gauntlet in the name of science or the

name of feeling, before the whole world.
Young eagles try to fly with a cloud above
them and an abyss underneath. Even the
most common man, before learning that he is
a turtle, has moments in which he thinks himself an eagle.

In such a condition was Yosef, and in this
case there was simply no one with whom to be
at sword's-points.

In the University he had a greater or less
number of adherents, a field in the wide world
might open, but Yosef did not know this wide
world yet.

Suddenly something happened which snatched
him from his lethargy.

Augustinovich had acted in a way that
offended the honor of students. They determined to expel him.

That was not his first offence, but the
students had always passed those matters over
among themselves, not wishing to be com-
promised in public opinion; now the measure
had been exceeded. We will not acquaint the
reader with the offence; what concern have we
with foulness? It is enough that a court composed of students had decided to expel the
offender. From such decisions there was no
appeal, for the University authorities always

confirmed them ; an appeal would only make it known more widely.

Indignation among students was great; no one took the part of Augustinovich except Yosef, who rousing half the University exerted his power to save the man.

" You wish to expel him," said he, at a very stormy meeting. " You wish to expel him? But do you think that after he has left the University he will not bring shame to you? What will he do with himself? Where will he go? How will he find means of living? How will he maintain himself? And do you know why he fell? No! — Ask him when he has eaten a dinner. We are among ourselves. Raise either of his feet, the right or the left, all the same! If under his boots you find one sound sole, expel him. As to me I declare, and may the thunderbolts split any one who will say otherwise, that we ought to save, not to ruin the man. Give him salvation, give him bread — take him on your own responsibility ! "

"Who will answer for him ? " asked one of Augustinovich's opponents.

" I ! " shouted Yosef in a thundering voice; and he threw his cap on the floor.

There was uproar and confusion in the room. Vasilkevich supported Yosef with all his influence, others insisted on his expulsion, there was no " small uproar." Yosef sprang onto a bench, and turning to Augustinovich shouted, —

" They forgive thee ! Come with me."

He left the room, rubbing his hands with internal delight, and cried, —

" It would be a pity to lose such a head ! Besides, let them eat the devil if they act without me now ! "

"Why didst thou save me?" inquired Augustinovich.

Yosef turned a severe face toward him and said, —

" To-day thou wilt move into my lodgings."

Meanwhile another drama was played in Pani Helena's lodgings. She was a most peculiar person; she could not exist, she knew not how to exist, without attaching her life to some feeling. Her first chance had been fortunate; she proved a model wife and mother. It had seemed to her that she found salvation in Yosef, and now months had passed since she had seen him; and she desired him the more, the more persistently Gustav resisted.

The last struggle of these directly opposing forces had to come.

" If thou wilt not return him to me," said

the widow in tears, one evening, "I will go myself to find him. I am ready to kneel down before thee and beg on my knees for him, Gustav! Thou sayest that Kazimir begged thee to have care over me; so I implore thee in his name. O God, O God! Thou dost not understand that it is possible to suffer; thou hast never loved, of course."

"I, Pani! have never loved?" repeated Gustav, in a very low voice; and in his eyes real pain was evident. "Perhaps thou art speaking the truth. Then thou hast observed nothing, hast seen nothing? I know not myself that I have loved any one except — O God, what do I utter! — except thee alone."

He threw himself at Helena's feet.

Great silence followed. One might have said that the two persons had become stone, — she bent backward, with her hands over her face, he at her feet. They continued in this posture, both oblivious of everything around them. But a moment comes when the greatest pain is conquered.

He rose soon, a new man; he was very calm. He roused her, and spoke in a low voice, interrupted through a lack of breath.

"Pardon me, Helena! I should not have done this, but thou seest I have been suffering so long. This is the third year since I saw thee the first time — I saw thee in a church; the priest was just elevating the chalice, and thou wert inclining — I visited that church afterward, I saw thee more frequently, and, pardon me! I myself cannot tell how it happened. Afterward thou didst become his wife — I said nothing. And this time I did not wish to offend or annoy thee, but thou sayest that I have never loved. Thou seest that that is not true. How hard it is to renounce the last hope! Pardon me! Pan Yosef will come to-day to thee — he is a man of noble nature, love him, be happy — and farewell."

He bent toward her, and raising the hem of her garment, with gleaming upturned eyes, he kissed the cloth as though it were sacred.

After a while the widow was alone.

"What did he say?" whispered she, in a low voice. "What did Gustav say? He said, I remember it, that *he* would come again to me. Am I dreaming? But no, *he* will come."

CHAPTER VI

MEANWHILE Augustinovich went to live permanently with Yosef. How different was his former from his present life! Formerly he had had no warm corner, now Yosef gave him a warm corner; he had had no bed, Yosef bought him a bed; he had had no blanket, Yosef bought him a blanket; he had had no clothes, Yosef got clothes for him; he had been without food, Yosef divided his own dinner with him. He found himself in conditions entirely different. Warmed, nourished, in a decent overcoat, combed, washed, shaved, he became a different man altogether. He was, as we have said, a person with a character unparalleled for weakness; conditions of life always created him, he was merely the resultant of forces. So under Yosef's strong hand he changed beyond recognition. He began to enjoy order and plenty, abundance in life. As before he had not been ashamed of anything, so now he began to be ashamed of everything which was not in accord with gloves and elegant clothing. Most difficult of all was it to disaccustom himself from drinking; but he had no chance to resume his former vice, for Yosef, who guarded him as the eye in his head, did not let him out of sight; he bought vodka for him, but did not let him have money. It would be difficult to describe the impatience with which Augustinovich waited for the moment when Yosef opened the cupboard to pour him a glass. How much he dreamed in that moment, how he represented the taste of the drink to himself, the putting of it to his lips, the touch of it on his tongue, the swallowing through his throat, and finally the solemn entrance of it into his stomach!

But Yosef, to deprive this treat of its humiliating character, drank to him usually.

In the course of time he treated him better; he began to associate him with various affairs of his own and the University, and finally with his own way of thinking. There is no need of saying that Augustinovich took all this to himself, that he repeated Yosef's words where he could preface them usually with, "I judge that, etc." Who would have recognized him? He, for whom nothing had been too cynical, said now in student gatherings when the conversation took too free a turn, "Gentlemen, above all, decency." The students laughed; Yosef himself smiled in silence, but so far he was content with his own work.

We need not add that Yosef attending the same faculty with Augustinovich studied with him evenings. He had then the opportunity of estimating the man's capabilities to the full. For that mind there was no such thing as more difficult or easier; a certain wild intuition took the place of thought and deliberation. His memory, not so retentive as it was capacious, took the place of labor.

Vasilkevich visited them frequently. At first he came with Karvovski, then he came alone daily at his own hour. His conversations with Yosef, circling about the most important questions of life and science, became more confidential. Those two men felt each other, and each divined in the other a strong mind and will. A relation founded on mutual esteem seemed to herald a permanent future.

Both seized in their hands the direction of youth in the University; the initiative of general activities started only with them, and since they agreed there was agreement in the University; comradeship and science gained most by that friendship.

"Tell me," inquired Yosef on a time, "what do they say of my action with Augustinovich?"

"Some pay thee homage," answered Vasilkevich; "others laugh. I visited one of thy opponents on behalf of our library; I found there no small crowd, and they were just speaking of thee and Augustinovich. But dost thou know who defended thee most warmly?"

"Well, who was it?"

"Guess."

"Lolo Karvovski."

"No, not he."

"As God lives, I cannot imagine."

"Gustav."

"Gustav?"

"Ah, he told those who were laughing at thee so many agreeable facts — they will not forget them soon, I guarantee that. Thou knowest how well he can do such things. They were astounded.

"I should not have expected this of Gustav."

"I had not seen him for a long time. Oh, he has sunk in that wretched love to the ears. But he is a strong fellow — and I am sorry for him. Tell me, thou art more skilled in this than I am: is he very sick?"

"Oh, he is not well."

"What is it? asthma?"

6

Yosef nodded. "Excessive work, grief."

"Too bad."

All at once steps were heard on the stairs, the door opened, Gustav walked in.

He was changed beyond recognition. The skin on his face had become wonderfully white, it had grown transparent. From his face came a certain coldness, as from a corpse; a yellowish shade shone from his forehead, which seemed to be of wax. His lips were white; his hair, beard, and mustache looked almost black as compared with that pallor. He was like a man who had passed through a long illness, and on his face had settled certainty concerning himself and a kind of despairing resignation.

Yosef, a little astonished, a little confused, did not know perhaps how to begin. Gustav brought him out of the trouble.

"I have come to thee with a prayer," said he. "Once thou didst promise not to visit the widow; withdraw that promise."

Yosef made a wry face with a kind of constraint. But he only answered, —

"It is not a custom with me to break my word."

"True," answered Gustav, calmly; "but this is something entirely different. If I were to

die, for example, the promise would not bind
thee, and I, as thou seest, am sick, sick very
grievously. Meanwhile she needs protection.
I cannot protect her now, I cannot watch
over her. I must lie down to rest, for I am
wearied somewhat. For that matter, I will tell
the whole truth to thee. She loves thee, and
beyond doubt thou lovest her also. I have
stood in thy way and hers, but now I withdraw. I do so perforce, and I shall not repre-
sent this as a sacrifice. I loved her much, and
I had a little hope that she would love me
some day; but I was mistaken." Here his voice
fell an octave lower. "No one has ever loved
me. It has been very gloomy in life for me —
But what is to be done? Of late I have passed
through much, but now that is over. To-day
my concern is that she be not left alone. Had
I been able to decide on a sacrifice, thou
wouldst be her protector to-day. Canst thou
do this for me, Yosef? Thou hast energy,
thou art rich, and she, I say, loves thee, so
thou wilt not end as I have. Oh, it has been
hard in this world for me — But never mind.
I should not like to do her an injury — I love
her yet. I should not wish her to be alone
because of me. At times, seest thou, it is not
proper to refuse people anything. Go, go to

her! Thou and I lived together once, we
fought the same trouble, hence thou shouldst
do me this favor; for, I repeat, I am sick
and I know not whether I shall see her or thee
again."

A tear gathered in Vasilkevich's eye; he rose
and said, turning to Yosef, —

"Thou shouldst do all that Gustav asks of
thee."

"I will go to her, I will protect her," answered Yosef, decidedly. "I give my word of
honor to both of you."

"I thank thee," said Gustav. "Go there
now."

A little later he was alone with Vasilkevich.
The Lithuanian was silent for some time, he
struggled with his own heart; finally he spoke
in a voice of heartfelt sympathy, —

"Gustav, poor Gustav, how thou must suffer
at this moment!"

Gustav made no answer. He drew the air
into his mouth with hissing, gritted his teeth,
his face quivered convulsively, and a sudden
sobbing tore his breast, strength left him
altogether.

.　.　.　.　.　.　.　.

Three days later Yosef and Vasilkevich were
sitting in Gustav's lodging. The evening was

bright; bundles of moonlight were falling into the room through the panes. At the bedside of the sick man a candle was burning. The sick man himself was still conscious. Almost beautiful was his face, which had grown yellow from suffering, with its lofty forehead, as it rested on high pillows. One emaciated hand lay on the blanket, with the other he pressed his bosom.

The light of the candle cast a rosy gleam on that martyr to his own feelings. The opposite corner of the room was obscure in the shadow. Gustav was giving an account of how he had cared for Helena. From time to time he answered, though with difficulty, now to Yosef, now to Vasilkevich, who, standing at the head of the bed, wiped away the abundant perspiration which came out on the forehead of the sufferer.

"I wish to forewarn thee," said Gustav. "They send her two thousand zlotys yearly (about $250), but she needs from five to six thousand. I earned the rest for her — Push away the candle, and moisten my lips — I took from my own mouth, I did not sleep enough — Sometimes I did not eat a meal for two days — Raise me a little, and support me higher, I cannot speak — There are thirty rubles more

for her in that box — It is dark around me —
Let me rest — "

A mouse made a piece of paper rustle in
one corner; except that, silence held the room.
Death was coming.

" I should like to finish our work," continued
Gustav. " Tell my associates not to quarrel —
Cold is seizing me — I am curious to know if
there be a hell or a heaven. I have never
prayed — but, but — "

Vasilkevich inclined toward him and asked
in a low voice, —

" Gustav, dost thou believe in immortality? "

The sick man could speak no longer; he
nodded in sign of affirmation. Then low tones
of enchanting music seemed to be given forth
in that chamber. Along the rays of the moonlight a legion of angels pushed in from the
sky ; the room was filled with them, some with
white, others with golden or colored wings.
They came quietly, bent over the bed. The
rustle of their wings was audible.

The spirit of Gustav went away with that
low-sounding orchestra.

The funeral took place with great solemnity.
The whole University in a body was present
around the coffin. Then they spoke for the
first time of the accurate knowledge, the toil

and sacrifices of the deceased. It appeared from the accounts which Yosef examined that Gustav had earned about four thousand zlotys ($500) yearly. All of this went to the widow; he lived himself like a dog. This voluntary but silent heroism made for him an enduring monument in the hearts of the young men. They discovered also various labors of the deceased which indicated solid acquirements, nay, talent. They found his diary, which was a confession in simple and even blunt words of all the dark side of his life of privation, a kind of apology for the passionate outbreaks of youth, those imaginary but still real sufferings, those struggles, those pains, those internal storms, and conversations held with self. The inner life of enthusiastic natures was unveiled there in all its dark solemnity. It was a terror to look into that chaos which is not to be known in every-day life, in that "so devilishly gilded world," as the poetess calls it.

The memoirs were read at Vasilkevich's rooms; there was even a proposition to print them, though it was not brought into effect somehow. But Augustinovich wrote a paper after Gustav's death. Very eloquently did he describe the man's career. He showed him from years of childhood, when he was still happy. The charm of the description of those spring moments of life was so great that it seemed as though the sun of May had shone upon the writer. Then the picture grew sombre. It was seen how the deceased had left his native cottage; how the dog, the old servant, ran after him howling. Then still darker: life hurled him about, tossed him, rent him. Again a ray shone as if on a cloud. In rainbow form Pani Helena appeared to him — he stretched his arms toward that light. "The rest you know," wrote Augustinovich. "Let him sleep now, and dream of her. The field swallow will sing her name above his grave. Let him rest in peace. The spark is quenched, the bowl is broken — that is Gustav."

But it happens usually that people after his death speak much of a man whom during life they almost buffeted. Let us give peace then to Gustav, and follow the further fortune of our acquaintances, and especially of Yosef, the hero of this volume.

With him nothing had changed, but he himself from the time of his first visit to Pani Helena went about as if in meditation and was silent.

Augustinovich accustomed himself more and more to the new condition.

At the general's the guests danced as before. At the engineer's they pounded on the piano. The countess sang in the evening. Gustav's room was occupied by a shoemaker who had two scrofulous descendants and a wife with a third misery. In the place where thoughts from a noble head had circled and words of warmth had dropped, were now heard the thread and the shoemaker's stirrup.

The widow did not hear of Gustav's death immediately; Yosef concealed it, fearing too violent an impression. Later he was astonished to find that she received the news with sadness, it is true, but with no sign of despair. We have much to tell of those new relations; in the succeeding part we shall pass to them directly.

CHAPTER VII

YOSEF, according to his promise given Gustav, visited Helena, and after the second visit went away in love. He returned late at night. The stars were twinkling on a serene sky; from the Dnieper came the cool, but bracing breath of water. Light streaks of mist wound in a long line on the east. There was music in the air and music in Yosef's breast. He was in love! It seemed to him that the serene night had visited his betrothal with happiness. Full happiness is both a remembrance and a hope. Yosef felt yet in his palms the small hands of Helena; he remembered that moment, thought of the tenderness of the morrow, looked forward to that coming moment. A wonderful thing! She took farewell of him with the word, "Remember;" but who could forget happiness, especially when the future is smiling with it?

He loved! Pressed by the power and the charm of the night, the trembling of the stars and the majesty of dark expanses, he cast a look full of fire to the remotest borders of heavenly loneliness, and whispered with quivering lips, —

" If Thou exist! Thou art great and good."

Notwithstanding the condition set up before this statement, that for Yosef was very much.

He recognized greatness and goodness. He said, "If Thou art." If those words had been spoken about some being, they would be conditional; spoken to some being they were an affirmation of existence: " Thou art."

In spite of all his realism let us not wonder so much at these words. The lips which pronounced them had drunk freshly from the cup of ecstasy.

When Yosef reached home, Augustinovich was sleeping in the best fashion possible; his snoring was heard even on the stairway. He drew out the song of slumber, now short, now long, now lower, now higher, now puffing, now blowing, now whistling.

Yosef roused him.

He determined finally to embrace him.

Augustinovich stared at him with astonished eyes, and at the first moment cried, —

" Go to the — "

Yosef laughed joyously.

"Good-night!" said Augustinovich. "I will tell thee to-morrow where thou art coming from — now I wish to sleep — good-night."

The next day was Sunday. In the morning Yosef poured the tea; Augustinovich, lying in bed yet, and looking at the ceiling, was smoking a pipe. Both were thinking of the day previous.

Finally Augustinovich was the first to speak, —

"Dost thou know what has come to my head?"

"No."

"Then I will tell thee. I will tell thee that it is not worth while to attach one's life to the first woman that comes along; as I wish well to Jove, it is not! There are better things in this world."

"Whence did those ideas come to thee?"

"Straight from the pipe. A man binds himself firmly to an idea, grows one with it, and then something comes and, behold! of those palaces as much remains as of the smoke which I blow out at this moment."

An immense roll of smoke rose from Augustinovich's lips, and striking the ceiling was scattered on all sides.

The conversation was stopped for a while.

"Yosef, hadst thou been in love before knowing Gustav and Pani Helena?"

"Had I lo-v-ed?" drawled Yosef, looking at the light through his glass of tea. "What? had I loved? Yes, I turned my head for a moment, but that did not push me out of life's ordinary conditions, it did not lead me out of the order of the day. I will say sincerely, though, that I have not been in love."

Augustinovich, raising the stem of his pipe, began to declaim with solemnity, —

"O woman! helpless down! O giddy creature!"

"Well, what is it?" asked Yosef, laughing.

"Nothing, my reminiscences. Ei, it was different with me. I was as mad as a maniac a couple of times. Once, even in spite of misery, I tried to be an orderly person; it was difficult, but I tried."

"And how did it end?"

"Prosaically. I was giving lessons in a certain house. There were two children, a little son and a grown-up daughter. I taught the son and fell in love with the daughter. I told her this one evening, and tears came to my eyes. She was confused a little, and then she laughed. Thou wilt not believe, Yosef, what an ugly laugh that was, for she saw how much the confession had cost me, and besides she had enticed me on, to begin with. She went at once with a complaint to her 'mamma.'"

"Well, what did the mamma do?"

"The 'mamma' told me first that I was a scrub, whereupon I bowed to her; second she told me to go my way, and third she threw a five-ruble note on the floor before me. I picked up the note, for it belonged to me, and from it I got drunk that evening and next morning also."

"And then?"

"Then the next evening and the third morning."

"And so on?"

"No. On the fourth day I had an immense cry, and later, when I had cured myself a little, not of drinking, but of love, I tried to fall in love with the first woman I met; but I could not love any more, I give thee my word of honor."

"And hast thou no hope for the future?"

Augustinovich thought a moment, and answered, —

"No, I have no respect now for women. As much as I believed in them before, as much as I honored and loved them as the highest reward of toil and effort, that much do I like them now, dost understand? That excludes love."

"But happiness."

"Not a word about happiness. So to-day I whistle when I want to cry, and therefore envy thee."

Yosef looked quickly at Augustinovich.

"What dost thou envy me?"

"Thy relation with Pani Helena. Do not frown, and do not wonder that I know those things well. Ho, ho! we have had a little experience. For that matter I will tell thee that I wanted myself to fall in love with Pani Helena. I prefer such women. Though, on the other hand — But do I know that thou wilt not be angry?"

"Talk on."

"I was afraid to fall in love with her. There is no denying that she is an unhappy woman, but, by the beard of the Prophet! what is that to me? I know only that the inheritance goes from hand to hand, and that whoso approaches her is happy for the ages. B-r-r! By my honor I should not wish to be the heir to such a legacy, even for a friend."

Yosef put the glass of partly drunk tea on the table, and turning to Augustinovich said coldly, —

"Yes; but since I am the executor of the will, be so kind as to speak of the inheritance more considerately."

"Well, I will tell thee in perfect seriousness not this, who or what the widow is, but what thou shouldst do. I speak disinterestedly. I speak even to my own harm. The affair is of this kind." Augustinovich sat up in bed. "I know thee, I know her; she will rush into thy arms herself. Initiative on the part of a woman — Ho! that is not good! Love must be a conquest. In a month thou wilt be sick of her, thou wilt be tortured and throw her to the devil. Yosef, I wish thee well — marry Helena while there is time."

Yosef frowned more than before, and answered abruptly, —

"I will do what I think is proper."

And really that little word "marry" had not come to his head yet. While kissing the widow's hands he had not thought of the consequence of the kisses. He was angry at himself, and at this more especially, that some one had reminded him of duties of conscience. A day later, two days later, he would have reminded himself of them beyond fail. The reminder coming from another took away from this thought the charm of spontaneous action which flows from love and made it constraint.

The evening of that day Augustinovich met Vasilkevich.

"Knowest thou that Yosef visits the widow now?" asked he.

"What wonder?"

"The woman is in love with him to distraction. Think what will come of that, and judge what Yosef ought to do."

"He ought to love her too," answered Vasilkevich, with his usual decision.

"Yes; and then?"

"Then let them marry."

Augustinovich waved his hand impatiently.

"One other question. How wouldst thou act with Pani Helena?"

"If I loved her?"

"Yes."

"I should marry her without hesitation."

Augustinovich stopped him, and with his hand on his heart began to speak in a tone of deep conviction, —

"Seest thou, I am much indebted to Yosef, for that matter thou knowest this best of all, I should like then to pay him honestly, — yes, to pay him with advice. He is in a strange position, and still, dost understand, there are

7

certain laws of honor which we may not break.
I should not wish that any man at any time
could say to Yosef, 'Thou hast acted dis-
honorably.' I say openly I should not wish
that. Thou canst do much, thou hast influence over him."

Vasilkevich, instead of letting himself be
persuaded, grew angry.

"But why push into affairs which are not
thine? Leave him freedom. It is only a little
while since he began to visit her. Ei! Augustinovich, does this come from thy heart? If
Helena is anything to thee, then may I — But
this is interfering — thou lovest to pose and
speak well-sounding words. Play no comedy!
Thou art making a sacrifice as it were by
losing lodgings through Yosef's marriage, but
that is mere levity. Thou art deceiving thyself without knowing it. Have no fear as to
Yosef; if thou wert like him, no more would be
needed. What hast thou to do with this matter?
Thou hast not tact to the value of a copper."

"Keep these lessons for thy own use! Then
thou wilt not interfere between them?"

"If this undefined relation were to last long,
I should be the first to try and persuade, and
finally to force Yosef to marry her; but to
interfere to-day would be stupid."

Augustinovich went home, greatly confused; a feeling of truth told him, however, that the Lithuanian was right, and that on his part it would be really meddling and a desire for posing, nothing more.

CHAPTER VIII

A COUPLE of months had passed, winter had passed, spring had passed, summer had come, and those relations had not changed.

Yosef loved Helena, she loved him, and their life flowed on in mutual forgetfulness of the future. But there was a shadow between them, a shadow thrown by chance. One summer day the widow tied under her chin the ribbons of a dainty blue hat, and covering her shoulders with a cape, she took Yosef's arm and they went out to walk.

The sun was shining, there was a little dust in the air, and the heat made itself felt on all faces, though the hour was about six in the afternoon. Multitudes of people were on the streets; many acquaintances greeted Yosef with a friendly nod; some, and among them strangers, looked around at our couple. Really they were a beautiful couple. Yosef had grown, he had become manly; his chin and the sides of his face were covered now by a splendid, ruddy growth, and his face had a serious expression, with a certain tinge of pride. The

widow looked exactly like a young betrothed.
The wind blew apart the ribbons of her dainty
hat, played with her white dress, and bearing
apart the cape, showed her slender form. Leaning on Yosef's arm gracefully, she delighted
in him and the sun and the air, and was as if
born into the world a second time. Yosef
looked more at her than at the people around.
We will not undertake to repeat the words in
that twittering of lovers, without meaning for
others, full of charm for themselves. But there
was more serious conversation; she, for example, begged him to take her to Potkanski's
grave.

"In the summer," said she, "there is much
shade even in the cemetery. And it is so
long since I was there; still I cannot forget
him. Thou takest his place, Yosef, but permit
me to pray for him sometimes."

It was all one to Yosef for whom or for
what Helena prayed; so he answered with an
indulgent smile, —

"Very well, remember thy dead; but love
the living," added he, inclining his head toward
her face.

A slight pressing of Yosef's arm to her breast
was Helena's answer. She looked him in the
eyes, then blushed like a girl.

Yosef covered with his palm the little hand resting on his arm, and — was perfectly happy.

They went to the cemetery, and on the way met Augustinovich; he was smoking a cigar and walking with two ladies, a mother and a daughter. Augustinovich had the daughter on his arm, the mother hurried on a little at one side; plumpness and finally the heat hindered her haste somewhat.

Augustinovich was eloquent evidently, for the young lady restrained her laughter at moments. While passing Yosef he blinked with one eye; this was to signify that he was content with the world and the order of the earth at that moment.

Yosef asked Helena about Augustinovich.

"I know him, though I do not know his name. When Kazimir died, I saw him near me, then he disappeared somehow from my eyes."

"He is the most gifted scapegrace whom I know," added Yosef. "But he told me that he was in love with my lady."

"Why tell me that?"

"Without an object, but it is a wonder how all are attracted to thee."

"My dear Yosef, that is the one thing that I brought to the world with me. Thou wilt

not believe how sadly the years of my childhood passed. Thou knowest not my history.
I was reared in a wealthy family, where the
master of the house treated me as his own
daughter. After his death I was tormented in
that house with every rudeness, till at last I fled
and came to Kieff, where an old and very kind
man took me into his care. He called me He-
lusia always, and petted me as if I had been
his own daughter. But afterward he too died,
without leaving me means of living. Then I
made the acquaintance of Kazimir. Thou wilt
wonder how I went to a students' club? I
lacked little of dying from shame, I assure
thee, when I entered the first time; but wilt
thou believe? I was hungry. I had put nothing in my mouth for two days. I was chilled
through, I knew not what I was doing, and
what it would lead to.

"Then Kazimir approached me. Oh! he did
not please me that time. He laughed and was
glad, but it grew dark in my eyes. He asked
at last if I would go with him. I answered
'Yes.' On the road he put a warm fur around
me, for I was shivering from cold, and finally
he took me to his lodgings. There, when
warmth had restored presence of mind to me,
I saw where I was, and I wept from shame

and disgrace. For, seest thou, I was alone in a man's lodgings, I was in his power. He seemed to be astonished at my weeping; then he was silent and sat near me, and when again I looked at him he had tears in his eyes, and was different entirely. He kissed my hands and begged me to calm myself.

"I had to tell him everything, everything. He promised to think of me as a sister. How good he was, was he not? From that moment of knowing him I knew no more of want. At parting he kissed my hand again. I wished to kiss his, my heart was straitened, I pressed it with my hands and wept real tears. Oh! how I loved him then! how I loved him!"

Helena raised her eyes, in those eyes gleamed great tears of gratitude. She was as beautiful as if inspired. Yosef's expression, however, was severe; his brows had come together on his forehead. The thought that he owed that woman's love to empty chance, to a vain resemblance, covered his face with a gloomy shadow.

Potkanski had gone to her by another road. That comparison pained Yosef. He recalled Augustinovich's words, and conducted Helena farther in silence.

They reached the cemetery. Among the

trees were white crosses, stones, and tombs. The city of the dead in the shade of green leaves slept in silent dignity. A number of persons were strolling among the crosses; among the branches a bird from time to time sang half sadly, half charmingly. The figure of the cemetery guard pushed past at intervals.

Helena soon found Potkanski's grave. It was a large mound surrounded by an iron railing; at the foot of the mound was a small grass-covered hillock. Under these lay Potkanski with Helena's child. A number of pots with flowers adorned the graves, at the sides grew reseda; in general, the grave kept neatly and even with ornament indicated a careful hand.

Yosef called the guard to open the railing. Helena knelt there with prayer on her lips and tears in her eyes.

"Who keeps this grave?" asked Yosef of the guard.

"This lady came; a gentleman with long hair came also, but now he comes no longer. He always paid for the flowers, and he also gave command to erect the iron grating."

"That gentleman is here now — last year they buried him," answered Yosef.

The guard nodded as if to say, "And thou too wilt dwell here."

"But this I beg to tell the gentlemen. In the city out there are trouble and suffering, but when any one comes here he lies peacefully. I think often to myself: 'Will the Lord God torture souls in that other world also? Is it little that man suffers here?'"

After a time Helena finished praying. Yosef gave her his arm again. Yosef was silent; evidently something was weighing on his heart. By design or by chance he led Helena along a path different from the first one. All at once, when near the gate, he pointed to one of the graves, and said in a kind of cold voice, —

"See, Helena, that man there loved thee during his life more than Potkanski, and still thou hast not mentioned him."

The day was inclining. Helena cast her eye on the object which Yosef had indicated. At the grave stood a black wooden cross, and on it were written in white the words: "Gustav — died year — day."

The evening rays painted the inscription as it were in letters of blood.

"Let us go from here; it is getting dark," whispered Helena, nestling her head up to Yosef's shoulder.

When they entered the city, darkness was beginning in earnest, but a clear night was coming. A great ruddy moon was rolling up from beyond the Dnieper. In the dense alleys of the police garden steps were heard here and there, from an open window in an adjoining pavilion came the tones of a piano; a youthful, feeble voice was singing one of Schubert's melodies, the tones quivered in the warm air; far, far out on the steppe some one was sounding the horn of a post-wagon.

"A beautiful night," said Helena, in a low voice. "Why art thou gloomy, Yosef?"

"Let us sit a little," said he. "I am tired."

They sat there, and leaning shoulder to shoulder were both somewhat pensive. They were roused on a sudden from meditation by a youthful, resonant voice, which said, —

"True, Karol! The greatest happiness is the genuine love of a woman, if it is an echo to the voice of a real manly soul."

Two young people arm in arm passed slowly near the bench on which Yosef and Helena were sitting.

"Good evening!" said both, removing their hats.

They were Vasilkevich and Karol Karvovski.

When Yosef parted with the widow that evening, he held her hand to his lips for a long time, and went home late, greatly agitated.

CHAPTER IX

But next day Yosef after a perfect sleep was quite calm; he even laughed at the previous day and at his own alarms and fears.

"Many pretty phrases are uttered," said he to himself, "but are they reality? Only a fool regrets happiness. Gustav is the best proof of this. What good is feeling, though the strongest, though the most manly, when purchased at the cost of life? Besides, I am little fitted for tragedy. I love Helena, and she me. What is that to any one? Augustinovich, rise, O scapegrace! tell me what hundred-tongued Satan has turned the head of some brown parasol by means of thee?"

"Didst thou see her face?" inquired Augustinovich, forcing himself to sigh.

"I did, and by Jove, it was like a freshly plucked radish — the mother looked like a bowl of sour milk. Well, art thou in love, old man?"

"Be quiet! those are very rich ladies."

"Both? How much has the daughter?"

"Who has counted such a treasure — but she will be richer yet."

"Richer — by a husband and children?"

"No; but the mother has come on a lawsuit, and dost know whom she is suing? Our neighbor the count owes her several thousand zlotys."

"From whom dost thou know all this? Art long acquainted with the ladies?"

"Only since yesterday. I became acquainted by chance: they inquired for the street — whither? I did not mind, 'pon my honor, but I told them that the weather was very beautiful, and asked if they would not walk with me. The old lady loves conversation dearly. I learned immediately who they were, and why they had come to the city. She asked me if I knew the count. I answered that I visit him daily, and that I would use my influence on the old man to pay what he owes her. I said also that I was a doctor of medicine, theology, and many other sciences and arts; that I have an immense practice in Kieff. Then the mother began to tell into my ear her troubles and the troubles of her daughter. I promised to visit them and to examine their case carefully."

"Of course. What did the daughter say to that?"

"She hung out the red flag on her face, but the mother scolded her for doing so, called on all the saints, and assured me of the unanimous assistance of those saints at the day of general judgment. Thou seest what I have won."

"Thou art an innocent."

"I shall visit them to-day."

"Whom? all the saints?"

"No, my new acquaintances. I will advise them both to marry."

"The youngest thee?"

"What dost thou wish, my dear? A man grows old; moreover, I think that we shall greet thee soon with a hairy palm."

"I have begged thee not to interfere between me and Helena."

"Very well. I will say only that Pani Helena is beautiful."

"Surely!" answered Yosef, with ill-concealed pleasure.

At that moment Vasilkevich appeared.

"I have run in a moment," said he. "Karol is waiting downstairs for me; we are going to the country together. Yosef, I have business with thee. Briefly, I did not wish to mix in thy love affairs, notwithstanding Augustino-vich's prayers, but this is dragging on too long. Tell me, what dost thou think of doing with the widow?"

Yosef had a pipe in his hand; this he hurled violently into the corner of the room; then he sat down and looked Vasilkevich in the eyes.

"Question for question," said he. "Tell me, what hast thou to do with the matter?"

Vasilkevich frowned, became somewhat angry; still he answered calmly, —

"I ask as one comrade may ask another. Helena is not of that class of women who love one day but not the day following. Besides, through the memory of Potkanski each of his colleagues has the right to expect an answer to such a question."

Yosef rose; in his eyes blazes of anger were flashing.

"But if I give no answer, then what?" cried he.

Vasilkevich burst out in his turn, —

"Then thou thinkest, my bird, that we are going to let thee dupe this poor woman, and not ask what thy meaning is? Satan take thee! Thou must answer to us for the honor of Potkanski's widow. I am not the only man who will inquire about it."

They stood some time face to face, eye to eye, each with a storm on his forehead, as if testing each other. Finally Yosef, though trembling with anger, was the first to regain self-mastery.

"Hear me, Vasilkevich," said he. "If some other man had done this, I should have thrown him out of doors. I am not of those who let themselves be regulated, and I do not understand why thou and others mix in affairs not your own. In every case this offends me. I will answer, therefore, thee and all who wish to mention the honor of Helena, that I will give account of that honor only to myself, that I shall not permit any man to meddle with my acts, and that thou and thine are committing a brutal, and for Helena a harmful stupidity, in no way to be explained by your taking her part. I have done speaking and I am going out, leaving thee time to meditate over what thou hast done."

Vasilkevich remained with Augustinovich.

"Well? Did not he give thee a head-washing?" inquired the latter.

"He did."

"Hei! wilt thou say, then, that he gave thee a head-washing?"

"He did."

"Thou hast acted stupidly; with him mildness was needed — that is a headstrong fellow."

Yosef went straight to Helena. He was excited in the highest degree; he could not explain Vasilkevich's act, but he felt that that third hand, interfering between him and Helena, pushed them apart instead of bringing them nearer.

When he entered Helena's lodgings, the door of her chamber was closed; the maid could not tell him what her mistress was doing. He opened the door. Helena was sleeping, leaning against the arm of a large easy-chair. Yosef stood in the doorway and looked at her with a wonderful expression on his face. She did not waken; her rounded breast rose and fell with a light measured movement. There is nothing gentler than the movement of a woman's breast; resting on it, it is possible to be rocked to sleep as in a cradle, or in a boat moved lightly by the waves. Every man has passed through that sleep on his mother's breast. The secret kingdom of sleep is revealed in woman by this movement only, which may be called blessed, so many conditions of human happiness move with it in the regions of rest. The movement of angels' wings must be like it. It lulls to rest everything, from the cry of the infant, to the proud thoughts of the sage. The head of a sage, sleeping on the breast of a

8

woman, is the highest triumph of love. Such thoughts must have passed through Yosef's head, for, looking at the slumbering Helena, he grew milder and milder, just as night passes into dawn; he inclined toward her, and touched her hand lightly with his lips.

Helena quivered, and, opening her eyes widely, smiled like a little child when the velvety kiss of its mother rouses it from sleep. That was the first time that Yosef came to her with a fondling so gentle and delicate; usually he came, if not severe, dignified; but to-day he had come to wipe out and forget at her feet the bitter impressions of the quarrel with Vasilkevich. He was seized gradually by the marvellous power of woman, under whose influence the muddy deposit of the soul sinks to the bottom of oblivion. But he was too greatly agitated not to let some of the bitterness which he felt a few moments earlier press through his words. He raised his head, looked into her eyes, and said, —

"Helena, it seems to me that I love thee very deeply; but the folly of people irritates my personality, challenges me. I should like to find strength in thee. Trust me, Helena, love me!"

"I do not understand thee," replied she.

He took her hand and spoke tenderly, —

"Still, thou shouldst understand me. I flatter myself that I am not second to Potkanski in love for thee, or in labor for thy happiness. But there is a difference between us. He was the son of a magnate, he could give thee his hand at once, surround thee with plenty. I am the son of a handicraftsman, I must labor long yet over thy happiness and my own. I will not desert thee now, but I do not wish that thou as my wife shouldst touch the cold realities of poverty, from which he disaccustomed thee. But I need thy love and thy confidence. Speak, Helena."

Helena said nothing; but she approached Yosef, and, putting her head on his breast, raised on him eyes full of childlike confidence.

"This is my answer, my good Helenko," said Yosef; and with a long kiss he joined her lips to his.

"This may be egotism on my part," continued he, "but forgive me. I did not win thee by service or suffering, I have done nothing whatever for thee. The vision of wealth with which Potkanski surrounded thee on the one hand, the devotion of Gustav on the other, would stand forever between us.

Let me deserve thee, Helena. I have energy
and strength sufficient, I will not deceive
thee."

Perhaps it seemed to Yosef that he was
speaking sincerely; but how much offended
vanity there was in his words each person
may divine easily after casting an eye on the
conditions in which Helena had lived up to
that time. If he had asked for her hand
immediately, those conditions would have
changed very little, and certainly not for the
worse, since in that case, sharing his lodgings with her, he would have rid himself of
Augustinovich and all the outlays connected
with that man. On the other hand, it is proper
to acknowledge that he kept the word given
Gustav with complete conscientiousness.
Nothing had changed with reference to
Helena. Yosef would have taken her at that
time in the same conditions in which she had
been for two years past.

Beyond doubt one half was true in what he
had told her of his ambition; more meaning
still was there in his wish to throw down the
gauntlet to opponents; but perhaps the weigh-
tiest reason of all why he did not marry Helena
was found in the relations of great intimacy
between them of people not united by bonds

which give more than the right to fondling and
kisses. The cup was half drunk. Legalization
would lessen the charm of forbidden fruit,
would decrease sweetness already tasted, more
than it would promise new.

It will appear that Augustinovich was right
in some degree.

Yosef perhaps did not acknowledge to himself that his reason for not desiring to change
those relations was because he lived agreeably
in them.

Did he not love Helena, then?

He loved her; otherwise he would not have
visited her daily, he would not have kissed
her lips, her forehead, her hands; but let us
remember that this met just half the desires
which in other conditions we satisfy through
the way of the altar. The idea of a betrothed
is that of a woman disrobed behind a thin
veil, we go to the altar to remove the veil;
when the veil disappears a part of the charm
is lost. Honest human nature recompenses
the loss by the idea of attachment; when
attachment fails, habit, a thing still less en-
ticing, appears in the place of it.

But life rolls on.

Yosef had touched the veil; two ways led
to its removal, — one the way of the altar; the

other a momentary oblivion of self, a victory of passion over honor,—a less honest, in fact a dishonest, way, but short and alluring.

The first was difficult; to the second every moment was a temptation, every kiss an incitement. To the first the unfortunate guardianship over Helena disinclined him; selfishness counselled the second. But the first was honorable, the second was not.

Yosef stood at the parting of the roads.

It might be said, indeed, that an honest man should not hesitate; but we may also inquire how an honest man is to act when the powers of temptation are absolutely greater than his powers of honesty.

Helena loved Yosef; she answered nervously to his kisses. She was unable to turn the balance consciously; unconsciously she added to the weight of that defect which in Yosef's soul weighed against honesty and honor.

How many great and small battles, torments and terrors, that magic little word *love* brings with it sometimes! A whole rabble of wishes with outbreak and uproar, armed with goads and bells, a rabble capricious, violent, flies up from every direction, plays with the human heart as with a ball, hurls it to the lofty stars, or tramples it on the earth. Then, O man, all the dens of thy soul are thrown open. Thou hadst not even dreamed of what dwelt in them. All the seven deadly sins, and all the virtues of which the catechism makes mention, are fighting each other to win thee; thou seest thyself to be different from what thou hadst supposed up to that time; thou ceasest to trust thyself, suspectest thyself at every step, losest control of thyself. Passions rise up then like flames from the depth of thy being, and like hidden currents in a swamp, advance, creep, circle about, flow up, and then vanish.

The night of thy soul is rent by the flame of passions. In their colors thy own interior is shown to thee. Thou performest the rôles both of actor and audience. Thou art like a boat, without a rudder in billows of fire. Then, on a sudden, one thunderbolt finishes everything; the flames vanish like fireworks, and thou art dreaming, like Dante, of heaven and hell.

It is gloomy when after the awakening there is no one to give back the moments through which thou hast suffered. Calmness returns, but happiness returns not. An amputated arm gives no pain, but it does not exist.

It may be that Augustinovich had some truth on his side, when he said that it was not worth while to give life for a single feeling. Perhaps a man should not break himself against the narrow walls of personal whims and desires.

Above and around us is a broad world; waves are roaring there which have been raised by the whole of humanity. Is it not better to weigh anchor and push one's ship forth from the shore, quiet the weeping heart, and sail out into a future, without happiness but with labor, without faith but with thought?

It is certain that till the time of such a fiery test comes it is not possible to speak of the nobility of the metal out of which the soul of a given man has been cast. We can offer no guarantees, therefore, for the future acts of Yosef. He passed through various temptations, we know that; we guarantee that he fought with them according to his power; but how it ended, whether he or they proved the stronger, will be told later on.

CHAPTER X

ON reaching home Yosef met the old count and his daughter on the steps at the door. The young lady cast a glance of inquiry on him, and when she had gone a couple of steps, she looked around and smiled. Yosef noticed that she was very shapely, and with genuine satisfaction he heard her say to her father, "That is the young doctor, papa, who lives in the rooms under ours." It is true that he lacked little of finishing his course at the University; still he was glad that they considered him a doctor already.

Yosef's lodgings were open; the house guard was putting them to rights. From him Yosef learned details of the old count and his daughter. This man did not like either of them; he emphasized their stinginess, though he imagined that they must be very poor, because they did not pay room rent very regularly. "The young lady is haughty," said he; "all day she does nothing but play and sing. It is hard for her without a hus-

band, but what is to be done?" He did not
advise Yosef to make their acquaintance.

"How proud these people are," said he;
"but in their pockets, dear lord, there is
emptiness."

"And is the old countess long dead?" inquired Yosef.

"About three years. They have been rich,
I suppose, but he lost his property in wheat
which, as they say, he had to furnish in com-
pany with others at Odessa. That business
impoverished many people. The old countess
was better than others of her family. She was
an honorable lady, but she fell to grieving, and
died. They have lived here five years."

"Do they know many people?"

"It must be that they do not, for I have
not seen any one visit them."

Yosef, while waiting for Augustinovich, lay
down on the bed, and when he commanded
to bring him a glass of tea, he fell asleep
quickly. When he woke up, he felt a trifle
ill. Augustinovich had not come yet, though
it was quite dark. He arrived at last in
perfect humor.

The lady with whom he had become acquainted, Pani Visberg, had a daughter Malinka. Augustinovich examined them both

by auscultation. He prescribed dancing for the daughter and horseback riding for the mother. Besides, he promised to visit them and to bring Yosef.

"The old lady said that the summons to the count was ready, which does not concern me," said Augustinovich. "She has even visited the count, but found only the countess, who pleased her. The countess was much frightened when she learned the object of the old lady's visit. I asked Pani Visberg why she claimed a miserable two thousand when she represented herself as the wife of a Crœsus. She answered that her late husband's name was Cleophas, not Crœsus. 'If it were mine,' said she, 'I surely would not annoy them, but all that money belongs to my child.' Then I pressed the hand of that child under the table, with real feeling. I was simply moved — word of honor, I was moved. When going, I kissed the old lady's hand. The young lady's name is Malinka — a pretty name, Malinka, though the point is not in this, whether her name is pretty or ugly — Why art thou so pale, Yosef?"

"I am not entirely well, and I cannot sleep. I fell asleep while waiting for thee. Give me a glass of tea."

Augustinovich poured out the tea, and lighting his pipe lay on the bed. Yosef pushed an armchair up to the bureau, and taking a pen began to write.

He soon stopped, however. Thoughts crowded into his head; he leaned back in the chair and gave them free course. Another man would have dreamed. Yosef collected and summed up his own past; he thought over the conditions in which he was then, he cast up the future. Regarding this future, it was difficult for him to remain in the rôle of a cool reasoner. The words "That is the young doctor, papa," came to his memory involuntarily. To be a doctor and to some extent a high-priest of science; to rule on one side by reason, on the other by significance, property, reputation, — Yosef had not become indifferent yet to reputation, — to attract glances, rouse laughter, win hearts — Here he remembered Helena. In the region of feeling he was not free now to choose. He felt bound; still he would like to see eyes turning to him, and the smile of the maiden's lips, and hear the words so prettily whispered, "That is the young doctor." For the first time he could not free himself of the thought that Helena might be a hindrance to his campaign of advancement. He determined

to settle with that thought. Her education
was not in the way, she was educated; she was
twenty-one years of age, he twenty-four — the
difference, though too small, did not constitute
a hindrance. What reasons could he have to
fear that Helena might be a weight on him
some time? Conscience declared that the first
cause was his own vanity. He knew women
little, and he wanted to know them much and
to rule them. But there were other considera-
tions which Yosef did not admit. He loved too
little. In his soul lay enormous capitals of
feeling; he had barely offered a small part of
them in the name of Helena. He bore within
him a dim consciousness of his powers; that
foreboding deprived him of rest. He wanted
to reach the foundation of things, but it was
not easy for even such a self-conscious head
as Yosef's to reach final results.

Besides, he did not know himself whether
possible future triumphs were equal in value to
Helena. To have near him for all future time
a woman so charming and loving was the same
as to seize in its flight a winged dream of happiness shooting by, but if besides he knew how
many of those coming triumphs would be of
tangible value, how many would deceive him,
how many faces there were before him, he

would not hesitate in the choice. But he had not met deceit face to face yet.

Such meditations wearied Yosef. The lamp in the room grew dim, he began to doze. Some sudden knocking above roused him again. "They are not sleeping up there, either," thought he. He remembered the countess and her gladsome smile. "How lightly and calmly such a girl must sleep! But there is some truth in this, that girls are like birds. A man toils and labors and meditates, and they — But that one upstairs is quite a pretty bird. I should like to see her asleep. But it is late now, half-past one, and I — What is that?" He sprang quickly to his feet.

A violent pulling at the bell brought him to his senses perfectly. He opened the door, and raising the lamp saw the countess before him. She was as pale as a corpse; she held a candle in one hand, with the other she protected the flame of it. She wore a cap, and a dressing-gown through which her neck and bosom were visible.

"Pan Doctor!" cried she, "my father is dying!"

Yosef, without saying a word, seized his medicine case, and enjoining on Augustinovich to hurry upstairs with all speed, he ran himself after her. In the first chamber was the small bed of the countess, with the blanket thrown aside, and left just a moment before; in the next room lay the count. He was breathing or rather rattling loudly, for he was unconscious; there was bloody foam on his lips, and his face was livid.

In a moment Augustinovich ran in, uncombed and hardly dressed. Both occupied themselves with the sick man without regard to the young girl, who had knelt at the foot of the bed, and was nearly unconscious.

All at once Yosef and Augustinovich looked each other in the eyes; both had seen that there was not the least hope.

"O my God! my God! Call in some one else, perhaps," burst out the countess, in tears.

"Run for Skotnitski," cried Yosef.

Augustinovich ran, although he felt certain that on returning with the doctor he would not find the count among the living.

Meanwhile Yosef, with all energy and presence of mind, worked at the patient. He bled him; then, looking at the clock, declared that the attack was over.

"Thank God! There is hope then?" cried the countess.

" The attack is over ! " repeated Yosef.

Meanwhile Augustinovich came with the doctor.

Doctor Skotnitski declared that the sick man was saved for that time, but without ceremony he added that in case of a second attack death would follow unfailingly. He commanded to watch the sick man and not leave him for an instant. Our friends sat all night at his bedside.

Next morning early the count regained consciousness and asked for a priest. Augustinovich had to go for one. He brought some parish priest or chaplain, who read the usual prayers and litany, then heard the sick man's confession, gave him communion, and anointed him with holy oil.

For a number of hours the count was conscious; he spoke with Yosef, blessed his daughter, spoke of his will, in a word, did everything which is usual when people are dying in a Christian and honest way of going from this world to the other. The whole day passed in these ceremonies. When dusk came Yosef persuaded the countess to take some rest; for the poor girl, though of a firm constitution, was barely able to stand on her feet from watching and suffering.

She resisted long, and agreed only when he almost commanded her to do so. When leaving the room she gave her hand, thanking him for his care of her father. Yosef looked at her more carefully then. She might have been twenty, perhaps even less, for her well-developed form caused one to consider her older than she was really. She had a large but agreeable mouth, blue, clever eyes, and dark hair. In general, her face was uncommonly sympathetic. She had a beautiful forehead shaded with hair; the expression of her face, and her movements indicated a developed aristocratic type of beauty. Moreover, she had very small hands.

The count fell asleep an hour after she had gone out. Yosef and Augustinovich sat by a shaded lamp; both were wearied and thoughtful. Augustinovich spoke first in a low voice, —

" Tell me what will become of the countess when he — " He indicated with his head the sick man, and closing his eyes drew a finger along his throat.

"I am thinking of that myself," replied Yosef. "Perhaps some one of the family may be found."

" But if he is not found?"

"It will be necessary to talk with her. They are poor, evidently; the guard told me that their rent is not paid yet. But it cannot be that they have no blood relatives somewhere, or at least acquaintances."

"Well, in every case speak of this later," said Augustinovich, who did not like to dwell long on one subject.

"Wait," interrupted Yosef; "at least one idea comes to my head. So far no one has been here, and it is impossible that that poor girl"— he indicated with his eyes the room where the countess was sleeping — "impossible for that poor girl to stay here alone after his death. Tell me, is thy acquaintance, Pani Visberg, a pious woman?"

"As pious as a chalice cover!"

"Honest, simple?"

"In an unheard-of degree: but what connection has that with the countess?"

"I wish to place the countess in her care."

"But the lawsuit?"

"Just because of that."

Here the sick man moved suddenly. Yosef looked at him quickly, then whispered, —

"One instalment of rent stands in my way, but this and that may be arranged, perhaps something can be done after his death."

"Oi, rent, rent!" whispered Augustinovich. "To keep us awake I must tell thee a little tale. I have never paid rent, I was enraged whenever rent was even mentioned, and I never could accustom any house-owner to refuse taking it. At last I succeeded with one. He was an old little fellow, and stupid as the ears of Midas. Well, once I was sitting in a small garden which belonged to him, and because the season was summer and the time night, for want of a better occupation I was counting the stars in the sky. I was dreaming somewhat; a starry night, as thou knowest, brings a dreamy state of mind. Thereupon that ass came to me and spoke absurdly. He simply wanted me to pay him. I rose from my place, and outlining in solemnity with my hand a bow between the east and the west, I asked mysteriously, —

"'Dost see this immensity and those millions of the lights of God?'

"'I see,' answered he, frightened somewhat by the tone of my inquiry; 'but —'

"'Silence!' said I, in an imperious voice. And removing my hat I raised my eyes, and looking at the astonished man I thundered, —

"'Useless dust! compare thy five rubles—'"

On a sudden a suppressed groan interrupted

Augustinovich. The count had become livid, he was twisted up, the fingers of his hands were balled into lumps; the second attack had come evidently.

At that moment Yosef rushed to the sick man and straightened his arm almost by force.

"Ys! — Bleed him!" said he in a low voice.

There was silence. By a wonderful chance the lamp at that moment grew darker. From instant to instant was heard the quick low voice of Yosef, —

"His pulse? Water!"

"He is stifling," whispered Augustinovich.

Both held the breath in their breasts; the dull sound of the lance was heard. The steel sank in the old man's flesh, but blood did not come.

"This is the end! All is useless!" said Yosef, drawing a deep breath.

Drops of sweat came out on his forehead.

"He lived — he lived till he died," said Augustinovich, with the most indifferent mien in the world. "We have done our part, now to sleep."

CHAPTER XI

THE count died really, and was buried according to Christian ceremonial. After his death Yosef paid a visit to the old lady. It was a question of securing guardianship for the countess, since no one of the family had come forward.

The count had left very scanty means of maintenance, and even if he had left more the countess was too young to manage a house alone.

Because of the lofty piety and exceeding delicacy of conscience of Pani Visberg, it was not difficult for Yosef to arrange the business he had mentioned. He persuaded her that she had killed the count by her lawsuit, and therefore she was bound to give protection to the daughter of her victim. The lady was greatly terrified at the executioners of hell, with whom Yosef threatened her, and on the other hand she judged that the companionship of the countess, who was of society and highly educated as Yosef declared, would not be without profit to Malinka.

Pani Visberg was an honorable woman in the full sense of the word; she had not much wit, it is true, and still less acquaintance with society. The best proof of this was that she considered Augustinovich the acme of elegance, polish, and good tone. Yosef she feared a little, from the time of his first visit. But she was content in soul that such distinguished young men, as she said, were inclined to her lowly threshold.

Malinka, who in many regards resembled her mother, was seriously smitten with Augustinovich. She had induced the old lady to take a permanent residence in Kieff; for that matter Pani Visberg had come to the city somewhat with that intent. She wished to show her daughter to the world, for Malinka was nineteen years of age, and during those nineteen years she had been once in Kieff, once in Jitomir, and had sat out the rest of the time at home. Fortune permitted a residence in the city. The late Pan Visberg had been in his day an official in the custom-house, though in a funeral speech over his grave these words had been uttered: " Sleep, Cleophas Visberg! for during long ages the nations (all Europe) will admire thy integrity and stern rectitude." We say Cleophas Visberg left to his wife, inconsolable in her sorrow, about nine times one hundred thousand zlotys, and he would have left more if inexorable Fate had not cut short his days. He entered the kingdom of shadows more sated with years than with income.

But this income fell to good hands, for both ladies had excellent hearts. They helped widows and orphans; they paid their servants, male and female, regularly; they paid tithes to their church faithfully; in a word, they performed all Christian deeds which concern soul and body.

They received the countess with open arms, and with as much cordiality as if they had been her relatives. Malinka, an honest though simple maiden, was in love out and out with the noble orphan. How much she promised herself from the first glance to be kind and obliging to her, how much she wished to comfort her, how much she dreamed of a pure friendship with her in the future, it would be difficult to tell; enough that Yosef found as good protection for the countess as if she had been in the house of her own parents — it could not have been better.

It is true that the countess was well fitted to rouse sympathy. The silent and deep sorrow which weighed her down at the moment did not remove her so far from reality that she could not be charming to those who were kind to her. She thanked Yosef with tears in her eyes; stretched to him a hand, which he, with emotion rare in him, pressed to his lips. "As I love God!" said Augustinovich, "I almost wept when she looked at me. May the devils take me if she is not a hundred times more beautiful than I am."

In fact, that new figure, attended already with words of sympathy, had connected itself with the fate of the heroes of this book. That a countess like her could not remain without influence on them is understood easily. Whether the future will attach angel wings to the shoulders of the countess, or show in her charming body a barren, hypocritical soul, the continuation will teach us.

Hei! hei! If this life resembled a book; if it were possible to give people souls such as are created in thought; but then would these be people like the rest of mankind? It would be all one, however, for poison cakes are the food of this world, as the boy said. The human soul is like a spring; it carries poison far, and what man can guarantee that poison is not lying at the bottom of his own soul, and

that he would not create poisoned characters?
The soul is blank paper! God writes on one
side, and Satan on the other; but God and
Satan are only symbols in this case. In fact,
there is another hand; the world is that hand
really. The world writes on the soul, good
and bad people write on it, moments of happiness write there, suffering writes more en-
duringly than all. But there are souls like
mussels. The mussel changes grains of sand,
and the soul pain, into pearls; sadness and
solitude are the means. But not always. It
depends on the soul. Sadness and solitude
sometimes conceal weariness, emptiness, and
stupidity. These three full sisters like to dwell
in palaces built of sadness and solitude, seeking that which they have never lost. It does
not follow from this that there are no charms
in solitude. There are none in sadness, at least
for a sad person. Solitude for the soul is something like a time of sleep for the body. Nay,
more; that misty monad, the soul, seems to
dissolve in solitude, to separate, to vanish, to
cease its existence almost; words and thoughts
end in that silent region; the soul is annihi-
lated for a season, separates on all sides from
its own centre. All this is called rest.

Solitude is the worst term that the human

mind has had wit to invent; solitude is never alone, silence always goes with it.

It is a pity that the misty garments of this lady called Solitude are borne most frequently by that seductive page whose name is Laziness.

But sometimes, say the poets, solitude gives a creative moment. The soul is lost then and trembles, inclining to receive some vision flying in from beyond.

For this reason only fools or sages love solitude greatly.

What was the countess?

Let us see. It is time to descend from cloudy heights to life's realities. Let the countess enter! How? As a young maiden — can there be anything more charming under the sun? Such a beautiful mixture of blood, body, perfumes, flowers, sun rays — and what else?

Our illusions.

Fly in, golden butterfly.

CHAPTER XII

SAD, indeed, had been the previous life of the countess. During her father's life she had sat whole days in a chamber which was lonely and almost poor, listening to the twittering of sparrows outside the windows, or the quarrels of girls in the kitchen.

The old count came home every evening wearied and broken with ceaseless pouring from the empty into the void, as he called his affairs. Nothing succeeded with him. In his time he had been active and industrious; he had wished to give the aristocracy an example of how men with escutcheons should apply themselves to labor and industry, and as a result, he lost his property. There remained to him in return experience which he would have been glad to sell for a few thousand, and still one other thing which he would not have sold, that is, his reminiscences and his family pride.

In him the cement of that experience and that pride was his hatred of life, of men, of the whole world. This was natural. His own

people did not receive him, and those who did
receive the man, received him in such fashion
that the fable of the dying lion and the asses'
hoofs came to one's memory. If he had only
had a son! The young eagle might fly from
the nest with new strength, seeking light and
the sun — but a daughter! The old man did
not deceive himself: a daughter must become
either an old maid, or marry after his death
the first man who met her. For this reason
the count did not love his daughter as much
as he should have loved. In spite of that the
daughter loved him sincerely. She loved him
because he had white hair, because he was unfortunate, finally, because she had no one else
to love. Moreover, he was for her the last
volume of the story which she was weaving in
her mind.

Frequently in the evening her father told her
in his plaintive voice of the ancient deeds of
their family, full of glitter and glory, old his-
tories pleasant for counts and countesses; and
she while listening to them fixed her whole soul
in that past.

Often it seemed to her that from the golden
web of the legend some winged figure tore
itself free, half a hussar knight with a crooked
sabre in his grasp, an eagle-like son of the

steppe and of battle. He waved his hand, and the steppes were cleared of Tartars. One might say, "I can see the Crimea and the blue waves beyond." Hei! the usual dreams of a maiden! As wide as the steppes are, so many are the songs of his actions; and then he is so covered with glory, though youthful; so bloody, though so beloved. He bent his forehead before some female figure. The usual dream of a magnate's daughter! That female figure is she; he a Koretski or a Herburt.

And as she was reared, so did she imagine; and these imaginings had no use, nay, they were perhaps harmful, though attractive. So, when the old man finished the stories and, remembering the present, added with bitterness, "My fault, my fault!" she wound her arms around his neck, then, saying usually, "Not thy fault, papa; those times will return again."

But those times did not return. The old man died, and no knight appeared as a guardian, no knight cut from the blackened background of a picture. The form which appeared had nothing in common with knighthood. That head with severe face and broad forehead, the cold face of a modern thinker, in no manner, even in the dreams of a maiden, did it fit to a bronze helmet with ostrich plumes.

Other powers must have pulsated in the forehead of a man leading winged regiments against Tartars.

But, on the other hand, Yosef was something entirely new for the countess, something which made her admire. There were not many words in him, but there was force. In a short time he became for her everything; she found in the man decision, energy, and swiftness of action. Perhaps she could not explain to herself that that also was manhood, only different from the manhood of the past; or was she unable to discern that? The old count succeeded in nothing. Yosef when he had taken up her affairs did in one day more than the count had ever done in ten. He understood that the countess needed some resources, so as not to appeal in small things to the kindness and pocket of Pani Visberg. At this thought she trembled. He had foreseen it. He rescued radically the remnant of her income; and his acts in this regard were like the cut of a lancet, ever sure, always efficient. Naturally, Yosef managed by the aid of a jurist, an acquaintance, who, though young, would have talked love of God into Satan. But why did not the old count help himself in a similar fashion?

This brought the countess to a certain idea:

Aristocracy she imagined to herself in the person of her father, democracy in the person of Yosef. "Oh, what people they must be!" thought she, almost with dread, "terrible people who know how to crush obstacles, another kind of people." Books told the rest to her.

The countess went far in such thoughts. Once when she asked Yosef for details concerning his past, she heard him answer with perfect freedom, "My father was a blacksmith." She could hardly understand how he dared tell such a thing, so natural did it seem to her that if that were the case he ought not to mention it. Why did he not conceal it? These words were really a hammer which struck the soul of the countess most heavily.

She surveyed Yosef with an astonished glance, as if seeking a leather apron on him, or traces of sparks on his hands. Besides, it is proper to confess that, despite all her gratitude to him and Pani Visberg, she judged at first, in silence it is true, that the coronet inclined those people to her; she judged that in sheltering the daughter of a lord they did that somewhat to do themselves honor. But she learned that touching Yosef she was thoroughly mistaken. He pronounced the word count just as he did the word Jew, gipsy, or noble, not even turning attention to the special sense of those sounds.

Did he not understand? She could not admit that, though really the question of aristocracy lay thus far untouched in his mind. She suspected him, however, of ignoring it purposely. But that was not enough, — the countess noticed in Yosef's treatment of her a certain loftiness or rather indulgence. He was considerate and kind toward her, but in such a manner as if he wished to show that his action was the yielding of strength before weakness, the indulgence of a strong man for a child; though, on the other hand, how safe she felt under such protection!

It seemed to her as if there was nothing impossible to Yosef. She could sleep quietly and calmly; he was on guard. She tried, however, at once to relate herself to him differently; she wished to dazzle him with her culture. Meanwhile it came out that Yosef corrected her ideas gently, — showed her what was right in them, what was erroneous. Briefly, to her great disgust, he taught and enlightened her. She tried to impose by her talent, and on a certain occasion she sat down at the piano as if by chance and displayed cascades of melody before him; but what? That tormented Augustinovich sat down after her and played far better. This fellow also knew how to do everything, he knew everything!

The countess went in deep thought to her chamber that evening. But that she comprehended and understood these relations showed that her intelligence was not among the least, and it was not wonderful that she thought of these relations so soon after the death of her father, for even the very despair of a "well-bred" woman has in it a certain coquetry more or less conscious, though always innocent.

So a silent battle had begun between a new child of the people and an aristocratic young lady. It was developed by those relations which we have mentioned, relations which were barely tangible. This struggle was the more dangerous for him since he did not suspect it. The countess was not able to dazzle him, but she roused in him the most lively sympathy. For him she became a kind of beloved child whose fate he held in his hand, as it seemed to him.

Occupied with her actively, he neglected Helena; his visits to her became rarer. He pursued more the thought of doing something which might be agreeable to the countess than he fled before the thought of doing something disagreeable to Helena.

As for the countess, it is easy to understand that in her feelings for him there was not and could not be anything which contained hate in it. A somewhat roused vanity might lead rather to love than to hatred. To tell the truth, Countess Lula wished simply that that energetic democrat might in future bend to her aristocratic knees his submissive and enamoured head.

But she had not put the object clearly till she noticed that Yosef was a handsome man. We will state in parenthesis that Countess Leocadia was twenty years old, and that for some time there had been roused in her soul various yearnings and disquiets, of which she could not render account to herself. In the language of poets, that would have been called the echo of a desire " to love and be loved, and perhaps even to die young." But whatever the question was, we may be satisfied by knowing that it furnished Lula with a thread of continual thinking of Yosef, the confidence which she had in him. Her gratitude for protection experienced from day to day increased her sympathy.

It is true that the old countess in her time had told Lula that a well-bred young lady must not love; but Mother Nature whispered to her something quite different. In truth, those two mothers are often in disagreement. This is one reason why in the souls of most women a broad robust feeling rarely springs up and becomes vigorous in them; on the contrary, a thousand nervous little loves are planted, less winged, but less binding.

Lula verified the fact, then, that Yosef was intellectual, noble, and a handsome man; we will not dare to guarantee which quality it was that she emphasized most. That evening, however, when she was going to sleep she gave herself this question, which in the sequel was important, "But if he loved me?"

Instead of an answer she ran with bare feet and half dressed to the glass. Authors alone are permitted to see pictures of this sort. The night-cap was on her head, and from under the cap came to her white shoulders tresses of dark hair which disappeared under her night-dress. With gleaming eyes and moving breast she gazed at the glass. "But if he loved me," repeated she, "and if he were to kneel here pale and burning—" At that moment a blood-red blush covered her face and neck; she blew out the light.

Thenceforth peculiar changes began to appear in her; sometimes a strange disquiet mastered her, she fell into thoughtfulness; sometimes she walked as if drowsy, as if oppressed, weakened; at another time she covered her head on Malinka's breast, and kissed her without reason. Yosef she saw daily.

And so days and months passed; but by degrees some change began to take place in Yosef too. Gradually that dear child had ripened in his soul and become a beautiful woman in full bloom. His glance when he looked at her had not that former complete transparency and calmness. Formerly he might have lulled her to sleep on his breast, and laid her as he would a child on a couch; to-day that would have caused a surprisingly different sensation. The idyl grew stronger in the spirit of both, till at last, after so many and so many days, or so many and so many months, the following conversations took place in the lodgings of Pani Visberg and those of Yosef.

"If thou wert in love, Malinka?"

"Then, my Lula, I should be very happy, and I should love very much; and seest thou, my Lula, the Lord God would arrange so that the man should love me also."

"But if he did not love?"

Malinka rubbed her forehead with her hand.

"I do not know, I do not know, but it seems to me that there is a difference between loving and loving. I should love this way — O God! I do not know how to tell it — this way is how I should love — "

Malinka threw her arms around the neck of her friend, and pressing her to her bosom, covered her with fondling and kisses.

"My Lula, he would have to love me then."

And like two doves they hid their heads on the breasts of each other.

There was silence.

"Malinka!" said Lula at last, with tears in her voice.

"Lula, my heartfelt!"

"Malinka, I love."

"I know, Lula."

"Old man!" said Augustinovich to Yosef.

"What news?"

"May I be —— if this is new. Old man, I saw thee kissing the countess's veil. May I be hanged if thou didst not kiss it! Well, thou art fond of kissing — wait, I have a parasol here, perhaps thou wilt kiss the parasol; if that does not suit thee, then perhaps my last year's cloak. The sleeve lining is torn, but otherwise it is a good cloak. May I be!

—Give me the pipe—I know what this means, old man; that fool of a Visberg does not know, but I know."

Yosef covered his face with his hands.

Augustinovich looked at him in silence, shuffled his feet under the table, coughed, muttered something through his teeth; finally he said in a voice of emotion,—

"Old man!"

Yosef made no answer.

Augustinovich shook him by the shoulder with sympathy.

"Well, old man, do not grieve, be not troubled—thou art concerned about Helena."

Yosef trembled.

"About Helena. Thou art honest, old man. What is to be done with her now?—I know! If thou wish, old man, I will marry her. By Jove, I will marry her!"

Yosef stood up. Beautiful resolution shone on his broad forehead, and though on his frowning brows thou couldst read pain and struggle, thou couldst see that the victory would fall where Yosef wished it. He pressed Augustinovich's hand.

"I am going out."

"Where art thou going?"

"To Helena."

Augustinovich stared at him.

"To He–le–na?"

"Yes," answered Yosef. "Enough of deceit and hesitation! To Helena with a request for her hand."

Augustinovich looked at him as he went out, and shaking his head, muttered through his teeth, —

"See, stupid Adasia,[1] how people act."

Then he filled his pipe, turned on the bed, and snored with redoubled energy.

[1] Adasia is Adam, Augustinovich's own name.

CHAPTER XIII

HELENA was not at home. Yosef waited several hours for her, walking unquietly up and down in her chamber. He resolved at whatever cost to come out of the false position in which he had been put by his guardianship over the widow and over the countess, but he acknowledged to himself that this resolution brought him pain. That pain was great, almost physical. Yosef had come to ask Helena's hand, but it seemed to him at that moment that he could not endure her. He was rushing toward the other with heart and mind; thou wouldst have said that he felt a prayer in his own breast, that he begged of his own will for a moment more of that other. He loved Lula as only energetic natures can love who are apparently cold.

He prepared himself for the meeting with Helena, and he foresaw that it would cost him no little. There is nothing more repulsive than to tell a woman who is not loved that she is loved. That is one of the least possible hypocrisies for a real manly nature. Yosef on a time had loved Helena, but he had ceased to love her, even before he had observed how and how much he had become attached to Lula. When he saw this he had a moment of weakness ; he felt this new love, and he feared to think of it and confess it. When his heart spoke too loudly, he said to it: "Be silent!" And he closed his ears, fearing his own possible actions and especially decisions for the future. This was not in accordance with him, and could not last long.

Augustinovich with his peculiar cynicism cast this love in his eyes, and forced him to meet it face to face. Further evasion was now impossible. Yosef stood up to the battle, and went from it to Helena.

But he did not go without traces of a struggle. He had a fever in his blood, and he could not think calmly. Various pictures of small but dear memories came to his mind, wherewith at that moment he believed more than ever that Lula loved him.

"Have I the right to destroy her happiness too?" This imbecile thought roared in him like the last arrow of conquered warriors. He broke it, however, with the reflection that between him and Helena there was an obligation, between him and Lula nothing.

Other difficulties belonged to the result of
Yosef's decision. The decision was honest,
but still to turn it into reality he had to lie,
and then to lie all his life by pretending love.
Evil appeared as a result of good. "Ei, shall
I not have to go mad?" thought he. "And
this life will be snarled like a thread. Every one
is whirling round after happiness, as a dog after
his own tail, and every man is chasing it with
equal success." Ho! Yosef, who did not love
declamation, had still fallen into the dialectics
of unhappiness. Such a philosophy has a
charm: a man loves his misfortune as a happiness.

Meanwhile evening came, but Helena was
not to be seen. Yosef supposed that she must
have gone to the cemetery, and he did not
himself know why that thought made him angry on that occasion.

He lighted a candle and began to walk
through the room. By chance his glance fell
on Potkanski. Yosef had not known him, and
did not like him, though for the justification of
his antipathy he could hardly bring in the
words "lord's son."

When he looked again at that broad, calm
face, something glittered in his eyes which was
almost like hatred.

"And for her I am only the counterfeit of that man there," thought he.

These words were not true. Yosef differed altogether in character from Potkanski, and Helena loved him now for himself; nevertheless the thought pricked him, he would have given much if Helena had not on a time been the wife of that man there, and had not had a child by him. "And I shall have a child," said he, "a son whom I shall rear into a man, strong and practical."

"Ah, if that future child were mine and Lula's!"

He shook feverishly and pressed his lips; a few drops of perspiration glittered on his forehead. In the last thought there was a whole ocean of desire.

He sat in that way for half an hour yet before Helena came. She was dressed in black, with which color her pale complexion and blond hair came out excellently. When she saw Yosef she smiled timidly; but great pleasure was in that smile, for he had been a rare guest in recent times.

Happily for her, she had enough of tact or of feminine foresight not to reproach him; she did not dare, either, to rejoice aloud at his coming, since she knew not what he was bringing.

But the palm which she gave him embraced his hand firmly and broadly. That palm quivered with the heartfelt language of movements interpreting fear and feeling when lips are silent.

With a melancholy smile and hand so extended she was enchanting with the inexpressible charm of an enamoured woman. If she had had a star in her hair, she might have passed simply for an angel,—perhaps she had even the aureole around her head which love gives, — but for Yosef she was not an angel, nor had she an aureole; but he touched her hand with his lips.

"Be seated, Helena, near me, and listen," said he. "I have not been here for a long time, and I wish that the former freedom and confidence should return to us."

She threw aside her cape and hat, arranged her hair with her hand, and sat down in silence. Great alarm was evident on her face.

"I hear thee, Yosef."

"It is four years since the death of Gustav, who confided thee to me. I have kept the promise given him as well as I was able, and as I knew how, but the relation between us has not been such as it should be. This must change, Helena."

He needed to draw breath, he had to pronounce sentence on himself.

In the silence which lasted awhile, the beating of Helena's heart could be heard. Her face was pale, her eyes blinked quickly, as is usual with women who are frightened.

"Must they change?" whispered she, in a scarcely audible voice.

"Be my wife."

"Yosef!"

She placed her hands together, as if for prayer, and looked at him a moment with eyes wandering because of pressing thoughts and feelings.

"Be my wife. The time of which I spoke to thee before has come."

She threw her arms around his neck, and put her head on his breast.

"Thou art not trifling with me, Yosef? No, no! Then I shall be happy yet? Oh, I love thee so!"

Helena's bosom rose and fell, her face was radiant, and her lips approached his.

"Oh, I have been very sad, very lonely," continued she, "but I believed in thee. The heart trusts when it loves. Thou art mine! I only live through thee — what is life? If one laughs and is joyful, if one is sad and weeps, if one thinks and loves — that is life. But I rejoice and I weep only through thee, I think of thee, I love thee. If people wished to divide us I should tear out my hair and bind thy feet with it. I am like a flame which thou mayst blow. I am thine — let me weep! Dost thou love me?"

"I love."

"I have wept for so many years, but not such tears as I shed to-day. It is so bright in my soul! Let me close my eyes and look at that brightness. How much happiness in one word! Oh, Yosef, my Yosef, I know not even how to think of this."

It was grievous for him to hear words like those from Helena; he felt the immense false-hood and discord in which his life had to flow with that woman thenceforward, that woman so beautiful, so greatly loving, and loved so little.

He rose and took farewell of her.

Helena, left alone, placed her burning fore-head against a pane of the window, and long did she stand thus in silence. At last she opened the window, and, placing her head on her palm, looked into the broad, sparkling summer night. Silent tears flowed down her face, her golden tresses fell upon her bosom, the moonlight was moving upon her forehead and putting a silvery whiteness on her dress.

CHAPTER XIV

A FEW days later Augustinovich was sitting in Yosef's lodgings; he was working vigorously in view of the approaching examination. Loving effect in all things, he had shaded the windows, and in the middle of the room had placed a table, before which he was standing at that moment. Evidently he was occupied with some experiment, for on the table was a multitude of old glass vessels and pots full of powders and fluids, and in the centre was burning a spirit lamp, which surrounded with a blue flame the stupid head of a retort which was quivering under the influence of boiling liquid contained in it.

Work burned, as they said, in the hands of Augustinovich; no one could labor so quickly as he. With a glad smile on his face he moved really with enthusiasm, frequently entertaining himself with a song or a dialogue with the first vessel he took up, or with a pious remark on the fleeting nature of this world.

Sometimes he left his work for a moment, and raising his eyes and his hands declaimed in tones which were very tragic, —

> "Ah, Eurydice! before thy beauty
> I passed the rounds of success,
> And the sentence of Delphi was undoubted,
> That on earth I am the only one blest."

Then again in a hundred trills and cadences he sang, —

> "O piano! piano! — Zitto! pia-ha-ha-no!"

Or similar creations of his own mind on a sudden, —

> "And if thou fill a pipe, O Youth,
> And pressing the bowl with thy finger, put fire on it."

"By Mohammed! If Yosef should come, this work would go on more quickly; but he is marrying Helena at present — Ei! and as innocence is dear to me, I would fix it this way! Dear Helena, permit — And what farther? Oh, the farther the better — "

All at once some one pulled the bell.

Augustinovich turned toward the door and extending his hand intoned, —

> "Road-weary traveller,
> Cross thou my threshold."

The door opened; a man young and elegantly dressed entered the room.

Augustinovich did not know him.

The most important notable trait of the newly arrived was a velvet sack-coat and light-colored trousers; besides, he was washed, shaven, and combed. His face was neither stupid nor clever, neither beautiful nor ugly, neither kind nor malicious; moreover, he was neither tall nor of low stature. His nose, mouth, chin, and forehead were medium; special marks he had none.

"Does Pan Yosef Shvarts live here?"

"It is certain that he lives here."

"Is it possible to see him?"

"It is possible at this time; but in the night, when it is very dark, the case is different."

The newly arrived began to lose patience; but Augustinovich's face expressed rather gladness than malice.

"The owner of this house sent me to Pan Yosef as to a man who knows the address and the fate of Countess Leocadia N——. Could you give me some explanations as to her?"

"Oh yes, she is very nice!"

"That is not the question."

"Just that, indeed. Were I to answer that she is as ugly as night, would you be curious to make her acquaintance? No, no, by the prophet!"

"My name is Pelski; I am her cousin."

"Oh, I am not her cousin at all!"

The newly arrived frowned.

"Either you do not understand me, or you are trifling."

"Not at all, though Pani Visberg always insists that I am — But you are not acquainted with Pani Visberg. She is an excellent woman. She is distinguished by this, that she has a daughter, though it is nothing great to have a daughter; but she is as rich as Jupiter!"

"Sir!"

"Now I hear steps on the stairs, — Pan Yosef is coming surely. I will lay a wager with you that he is coming — "

Indeed, the door opened and Yosef walked in. One would have said that his severe and intelligent face had matured in the last few hours; in its expression was the calm energy of a man who had already decided on the means of advance in the future.

"This is Pan Pelski, Yosef," said Augustinovich.

Yosef looked at the newly arrived inquiringly.

Meanwhile Pelski explained to him the object of his coming; and though at news of the relationship of the young man to Lula his forehead wrinkled slightly, he gave him her address without hesitation.

"I take farewell of you," said Yosef, at last; "the countess will be greatly delighted to find in you a cousin, but it is a pity that she could not have found a relative two months ago."

Pelski muttered something unintelligible. Evidently Yosef's figure and style of intercourse imposed on him no little.

"Why give him Lula's address?" asked Augustinovich.

"Because I should have acted ridiculously had I refused."

"But I did not give it."

"What didst thou tell him?"

"A thousand things except the address. I did not know whether thou wouldst be satisfied if I gave it."

"He would have found the address anyhow."

"Oh, it will be pleasant at Pani Visberg's. Wilt thou go there to-day?"

"No."

"And to-morrow?"

"No."

"But when?"

"Never."

"It is no trick, old man, to flee before danger."

"I am no knight errant, I am not Don Quixote, I choose rather to avoid dangers and conquer than choose them and fall. Not Middle-Age boasting commands me, but reason."

A moment of silence followed.

"Wert thou at Helena's yesterday?" asked Augustinovich.

"I was."

"When will the marriage be?"

"Right away after I receive my degree."

"Maybe it is better for thee that the affair ends thus."

"Why dost thou say that?"

"I do not know but thou wilt be angry; but Lula — now, I do not believe her—"

Yosef's eyes gleamed with a wonderful light; he put his hand on Augustinovich's shoulder.

"Say nothing bad of her," said he, with emphasis.

He wished, indeed, that the countess, torn from him by the force of circumstances, should remain in his mind unblemished. He took pleasure in thinking of her.

"What am I to tell her when she asks about

thee?" inquired Augustinovich, after a short silence.

"Tell her the truth, tell her that I am going to marry another."

"Ei, old man, I will tell her something else."

"Why?" asked Yosef, looking him in the eyes.

"Oh, so!"

"Speak clearly."

"She seems to love thee."

Yosef's face flushed; he knew Lula's feeling, but that information from the lips of another startled him. It filled his breast with sweetness and as it were with despair together with the sweetness.

"Who told thee that?" asked he.

"Malinka; she tells me everything."

"Then tell Lula that I marry another from inclination and duty."

"Amen!" concluded Augustinovich.

In the evening he went to Pani Visberg's; Malinka opened the door to him.

"Oh, is this you?" said she, with a blush.

Augustinovich seized her hands and kissed them repeatedly.

"Oh, Pan Adam! that is not permitted, not permitted," insisted the blushing girl.

"It is, it is!" answered he, in a tone of deep conviction. "But — but," continued he, removing his overcoat and buttoning his gloves (he was dressed with uncommon elegance), "was some young man here this afternoon?"

"He was; he will come in the evening."

"So much the better."

Augustinovich went into the drawing-room with Malinka. The drawing-room had somehow a look of importance, as if for the reception of a notable guest. On the table a double lamp was burning, the piano was open.

"Why did Pan Yosef not come with you?"

"The same question from the countess will meet me. In every case permit me to defer my answer till she asks."

The countess did not keep them waiting long. She entered, dressed in black, with simply a few pearls in her hair.

"But Pan Yosef?" asked she at once.

"He is not coming."

"Why?"

"He is occupied. Building his future."

The countess was wounded by the thought that Yosef would not come.

"But do you not help him in that labor?" asked she.

"May my guardian angel keep me from such work."

"It must be very difficult."

"Like every new building."

"Why does he work so?"

"Duty."

"I believe that Pan Yosef builds everything on that foundation."

"This time it will be more difficult for him than ever before. But somebody is coming —that is your cousin. What a splendid man!"

Pan Pelski entered the drawing-room; soon after came Pani Visberg also.

After the greetings conversation began to circle about in the ocean of commonplace.

Augustinovich took little part in it. He sat in an armchair, partly closed his eyes with an expression of indifference toward everything. He had the habit of closing his eyes while making observations, when nothing escaped his notice.

Count Pelski (we had forgotten to state that he had that title) sat near Lula, twirling in his fingers the string of his eyeglasses, and conversing with her vivaciously.

"Till I came to Kieff," said he, "I knew nothing of the misfortune which had met our whole family, but especially you, through the death of your esteemed father."

"Did you know my father?" asked Lula, with a sigh.

"No, cousin. I knew only that unfortunate quarrels and lawsuits separated our families for a number of years. I knew nothing of those quarrels, since I was young and always absent, and if I am to make a confession my present visit was undertaken only as an attempt at reconciliation."

"What was the degree of relationship between you and my father?"

"Reared abroad, I know little of our family relations in general; for example, I am indebted to a lucky chance for discovering not our relationship, of which I was aware, but other intimate bonds connecting our families from of old."

"Is it permitted to inquire about this circumstance?"

"With pleasure, cousin. Having taken on me, after the death of my father, the management of my property and family affairs, I looked into the papers and various documents touching my family. Well, in these documents I discovered that your family is not only related to the Pelskis, but has the same escutcheon."

"To a certain extent, then, we are to thank chance for our acquaintance."

"I bless this chance, cousin."

Lula dropped her eyes, her small hand twisted the end of her scarf; after a while she raised her head.

"And for me it is equally pleasant," said she.

The shadow of a smile flew over Augustinovich's face.

"I had much difficulty in finding your lodgings. This gentleman" (Pelski indicated Augustinovich with one eye) "has a marvellous method of giving answers. Fortunately his room-mate came; he gave me an answer at last."

"I lived in the same house as they," added the countess.

"How did you become acquainted with them, cousin?"

"When father fell ill, Pan Shvarts watched him in his last hours; afterward he found Pani Visberg, and I am much indebted to him."

Augustinovich's closed eyelids opened a little, and the sneering expression vanished from his face.

"Is he a doctor?" asked Pelski.

"He will be a doctor soon."

Pelski meditated a moment.

"I was acquainted in Heidelberg with a professor and writer of the same name. From what family is this man?"

"Oh, I do not know, indeed," answered the countess, blushing deeply.

Augustinovich's eyes opened to their full width, and with an indescribable expression of malice he turned toward the countess.

"I thought," said he, "that you knew perfectly whence Pan Yosef came, and what his family is."

Lula's confusion reached the highest degree.

"I — do not remember," groaned she.

"Do you not? Then I will remind you. Pan Yosef was born in Zvinogrodets, where his father in his day was a blacksmith."

Pelski looked at his cousin, and bending toward her said with sympathy, —

"I am pained, cousin, at the fatality which forced you to live with people of a different sphere."

Lula sighed.

Oh, evil, evil was that sigh. Lula knew that among those people of a different sphere she had found aid, protection, and kindness; that for this reason they should be for her

something more than that cousin of recent
acquaintance. But she was ashamed to tell
him this, and she remained silent, a little angry
and a little grieved.

Meanwhile Pani Visberg invited her guests
to tea. Lula ran for a while to her own chamber, and sitting on her bed covered her face
with her hands. At that moment she was in
Yosef's chamber mentally. "He is toiling
there," thought she, "and here they speak of
him as of some one strange to me. Why did
that other say that he was the son of a
blacksmith?"

It seemed to her as if they were wronging
Yosef, but she felt offended at him, too, because he was the son of a blacksmith.

At tea she sat near her cousin, a little
thoughtful, a little sad, turning unquiet glances
toward Augustinovich, who from the moment
of his malicious interference filled her with a
certain fear.

"Indeed thou art not thyself, Lula," said
Pani Visberg, placing her hand on the girl's
heated forehead.

Malinka, who was standing with the teapot
in her hand, pouring tea in the light, stopped
the yellowish stream, and turning her head
said with a smile. —

"Lula is only serious. I find thee, Lula, in black colors — art thou in love? "

The countess understood Malinka's idea, but she was not confused.

"Black is the color of mourning; in every case it is my color."

"And beautiful as thy word, cousin," added Pelski.

After tea she seated herself at the piano, and from behind the music-rack could be seen her shapely forehead marked with regular brows. She played a certain melancholy mazurka of Chopin, but trouble and disquiet did not leave her face.

Augustinovich knew music, and from her playing he divined the condition of her mind. Still he thought, —

"She is sad, therefore she plays; but she plays because her cousin is listening."

But on the way home he thought more about Lula and Yosef than one might have expected from his frivolous nature.

"Oh, Satan take it, what will happen, what will happen?" muttered he.

In the midst of these thoughts he entered his lodgings. Yosef was not sleeping yet; he was sitting leaning on his elbows over some book.

"Hast thou been at Pani Visberg's?"

"I have."

Impatience and curiosity were quivering in Yosef's face; evidently he wished to ask about the evening, but on thinking the matter over he rested his head on his hands again, and began to read.

Suddenly he threw the book aside and walked a couple of times through the room.

"Thou wert at Pani Visberg's?"

"I was."

"Ha!"

"Well, what?"

"Nothing."

He sat down to his book again.

CHAPTER XV

A COUPLE of weeks passed. The relations of the personages known to us had not undergone change.

Yosef did not visit Pani Visberg's, but, to make up, Pelski was a daily guest there in spite of Augustinovich, who tormented him, and whom the count could not endure.

"How does the countess's cousin seem to thee?" asked Yosef of him one day.

"Oh, my friend, he is a zero."

"With what dost thou reproach him?"

"Nothing; what does stupidity mean really? He talks with the ladies as far as he is able; he wears a fashionable coat, glossy gloves; he knots his cravat symmetrically, praises virtue, condemns vice, says it is better to be wise than not; still, O Yosef, he is a zero."

"Thou judgest people in masses."

"Again! in masses. As is known to thee, I judge the breast according to the measure of the tailor, not that of Phidias; and as I advance laughter seizes me, but my heart does not burst, it must have cause sufficient to burst."

"Speak more clearly."

"What shall I say to thee? Well, he is a middling man, a man of the mean, but not the golden one; honest, for he has not done anything dishonest or perverse. But let him go! Better speak of philosophy or sing an old contradance; which dost thou prefer?"

"Let us speak of him, I beg of thee," said Yosef, with decision.

"Well, fill me a pipe then."

Yosef filled a pipe for him, lighted a cigar for himself, and began to walk through the room.

"I will not give thee an account of the evenings there, for I do not wish to annoy thee," said Augustinovich, "but if thou desire this thing, then listen.

"The affair is as follows: Pelski learned that the old count left a daughter, and curiosity led him to look at her. Seest thou, people are vain; they love effect, and the rôle of a rich cousin in presence of a poor one is not devoid of effect, so this rôle has pleased Pelski. Whom would it not please? Thou art wealthy, and givest thy hand to her (that is, to thy cousin), thou shieldest her with thy most mighty protection, astonishest her with

thy delicacy of feeling, with thy acts; thou
becomest her king's son — her ideal. Ei, old
man, how this tickles vanity! What romances
these are, Satan take me!

'O gray rye, he is digging the earth!'

It is a whole novel. A steed, a noble figure,
on her part smiles and tears — they are
separated by fate; later they meet, they
agree, they are reconciled, and Numa marries
Pompilius!"

These last words Augustinovich pronounced
with a certain maliciousness.

"Art thou speaking of Lula and Pelski?"
asked Yosef, gloomily.

"Yes; Pelski looked at her through curiosity, and she, as thou knowest, is a fair
maiden, and that rôle pleased him. Pelski is
an ordinary man, an aristocrat,— in one word,
zero,— but if she pays no attention to the
statue — "

"Yes, if?" interrupted Yosef, catching at
the last word.

"But thou — why deceive thyself? It must
be all one to thee. Thou art not a child nor
a woman; thou hadst full knowledge of what
thou wert doing when going to Helena with
a declaration."

Yosef was silent; Augustinovich continued:

"I say: Pelski is a young man and wealthy, she pleases him very much, and perhaps she will not look at the statue; she pleases him, — that is the main thing."

"Let us suppose that she will not consider the statue, what further?"

"In that case Lula will become Countess Pelski."

"Will she consent? What sayst thou?"

Yosef's eyes flashed.

"Listen, old man, I say this: I know not the good of this conversation. Perhaps she might not consent to-day, but in half a year or a year she will consent. If thou wert there thou mightest contend with him; otherwise, I repeat, she will consent."

"On what dost thou rest that judgment?"

"On what? A certain evening when I saw Pelski I was listening, and he asked, ' Of what family is Shvarts?' and she answered, 'I know not, really.' Thou seest! But when I said that thou art the son of a blacksmith, she was in flames, and almost burst into weeping from anger at me. There it is for thee!"

Yosef also felt at that moment as it were a wish to weep from anger.

"Seest thou," continued Augustinovich,

"Pelski unconsciously and unwittingly acts with great success; he brings her mind to ancient titles and brilliant relations; he cannot even do otherwise. And she is an aristocrat in every case. Thou rememberest how on a time that angered me and thee, and how much thou didst labor to shatter those principles in her. By the crocodile! there is nothing haughtier than proud poverty. Pelski acts wisely, he flatters her vanity, he rouses her self-love; that removes her from us. But we, my old man, are such counts as, without comparing— Oh, Satan take it! I cannot find here comparisons."

In fact, he did not find comparisons, and for want of them he fell to puffing out strong rings of smoke, and trying diligently to catch some of them on his fingers. Meanwhile Yosef looked stubbornly at one point in the ceiling, and asked at last,—

"Didst tell her that I was going to marry Helena?"

"No."

"Why not?"

"I said that thou wert toiling, and for that reason did not appear. Let the affair between thee and Pelski be decided in her mind, in her conscience and heart. Thy marriage is an external event which would decide the matter definitely on his side."

Yosef approached Augustinovich and fixed his fingers in his arm.

"Listen!" said he, violently; "but if I should win in this battle?"

"Go to the devil! and do not pinch me so hard. I throw the same question at thee: If thou shouldst win in this battle?"

They looked at each other, eye to eye; some kind of hostile feeling pressed their hearts.

At last Yosef dropped Augustinovich's arm, and hiding his face in his hands threw himself on the bed.

Augustinovich looked at him threateningly, then less threateningly, and still less threateningly; finally he pushed down to him and stroked him with his hand. He drew him by the skirt, and his voice now was soft and full of emotion.

"Old man!"

Yosef did not answer.

"My old man, be not angry. If thou win thou wilt preserve her in thy heart as a saint, and I will say to her: Go, bright angel, along the path of duty, as Yosef went."

CHAPTER XVI

HELENA hardly believed her own happiness. She was preparing for her marriage. Her clouded past had vanished, life's night was over, the morning was shining.

From a woman of a wandering star, who knew not where and how low she might fall, from a woman who was a beggar, from a woman without a morrow, to enter into a new period of life, to receive the affection of a man whom she loved, to become in the future a wife, to begin a calm life, a life which had a to-morrow, surrounded by respect, filled with love and duty, — that was her future.

Helena understood, or rather had a prescience of the abnormal relation between her past and her future. " From such a life as mine that ought not to come. I am not worthy of this happiness," whispered she to Yosef, when he placed the ring of betrothal on her finger. " I am not worthy of such happiness."

That half-insane woman possessed of love was right. Out of the logic of life such a future could not bloom, but her life had ceased already to move in its own proper orbit.

There are stars which circle in solitude along undefined orbits, till swept away by more powerful planets they go farther, either around them or with them.

Something similar had happened to Helena.

A stronger will had attracted a weaker. Helena met Yosef on her track, and thenceforward she travelled in his course.

The knowledge of this made her more peaceful. " Oh, if he wishes I shall be happy," thought she, more than once.

She had unbounded belief, not only in Yosef's character, but in his strength. So the last shadow vanished from her soul; alarm disappeared, that indefinite fear of the future which she could not dismiss till the moment of Yosef's declaration, this fear which tortured her like a reproach of conscience.

Her head was full of imaginings. With a song on her lips she made preparations for marriage, amusing herself like a child with every detail of dress. Notwithstanding her widowhood she wished to wear a white dress, which would also please Yosef. Regaining cheerfulness, she regained her health also;

she was busy, active, even minutely pains-
taking with reference to a future household.

She grew more beautiful and more noble-
looking under the influence of happiness.
From being a misanthropic woman, a bird
with plucked wings, she was changing into
a woman who felt her own worth, even in
this, that some one loved her.

The date of the marriage was approaching.

Meanwhile the time in which Yosef was to
become a doctor was drawing near. He toiled,
therefore, and toiled so intensely that his health
tottered. Sleepless nights and mental effort
marked his face with pallor; he grew thin,
blue under the eyes; he lived in continual
feverish labor, in reality he was losing his
strength, but he kept on his feet as best he
could, wishing at any price to win absolutely
both position and an independent future.

Besides ambition and the approaching date
of his marriage, one other thing urged him
to those efforts: the supply of money which
he had brought from home had been gradually
diminishing, and at present was almost exhausted. Now the burden of expenses and
housekeeping fell on Augustinovich. Augustinovich had given up drinking and earned
more than Yosef. Music lessons brought him

in very much relatively, and he did not need
to renounce them because of the pressure of
other work, for with him natural gifts took the
place of time and toil, even more than was
needed.

He went to Pani Visberg's daily, as before.
Malinka ran out every evening to open the
door to him, and every evening she snatched
away her hands, which he had the habit of
covering with numerous kisses. The honest
girl grew attached to Pan Adam. Did he
love her? Rather no than yes, for the past
had quenched in him the powers of sympathy.
In reality he had not fire to the value of a
copper. If passion had given heat to his
powers, they would have carried him far, but
the light from them was like moonlight, it
gave light without heat.

That, however, did not hinder him from
being, as they say, a capital fellow, a perfect
comrade, and a pleasant companion. If he
felt any attachment, it was for Yosef. But he
had his likes and dislikes; he liked Malinka,
but he did not like Lula.

And why did he not like her? There were
various reasons. She met him always with
cool loftiness, and besides she was a countess.
Usually he had success with women; he owed

it to his inexhaustible joyousness, and even to
his cynicism, which made him as if at home
everywhere. He had, moreover, a most particular power of adapting himself to that
society in which he chanced to be. Never
refined, he possessed (when he wished) high
social polish. He used to say of himself that
in him ease of distinction was inherited, since
it came "from worthy blood." He had never
known his parents, it is true, nor known who
they were. He had the hypothesis, even, that,
according to the well-known jest, Letitia the
grandmother of Napoleon III. and his grandmother were grandmothers; he proved in this
way his relationship with the Buonapartes.

Notwithstanding these characteristics, Lula
ignored him somewhat. Yosef's solid, simple
character roused a deeper interest in her than
the frivolous, elastic nature of Augustinovich.
Besides, she loved Yosef. So, by the nature of
things, Augustinovich remained at one side.
That annoyed him. This was the state of
things when Pelski appeared. Especially from
the time when Yosef ceased to pay visits, Lula
had changed uncommonly. Augustinovich annoyed her, for he judged things through the
prism of his particular repugnance toward her.
He thought that then, if ever, she would show

him dislike and even contempt; meanwhile it came out otherwise. Lula left her rôle of indifference and began to fear him.

"Thanks to the gods," thought Augustinovich, "a man's tongue is nimble enough, it seems. She is afraid that I shall make a fool of Pelski."

In fact, something of the kind happened a number of times, — a thing which it must be confessed touched Lula very disagreeably.

At first Lula asked about Yosef repeatedly, but received the same answer always, "He is working." At last she ceased asking. Still it seemed that she wished to win over Augustinovich. In her treatment of him there was now a certain mildness joined with a silent melancholy. Often she followed him uneasily with her eyes when he came in, as if waiting for some news.

This alarm was natural. Whether she loved Yosef or not, it could not but astonish her that he on whom she had counted so much, who had shown her so much sympathy always, had now forgotten her. She could not rest satisfied, either, with the answers of Augustinovich.

In spite of the greatest labor it was impossible that Yosef should not find in the course of more than two months one moment of time, even, to look in at her, to inquire about her health, all the more since she knew that he loved her. In this thought the coming of Pelski was connected in her mind wonderfully with the absence of Yosef. She supposed, justly, that there was a certain connection between them. Augustinovich alone could explain these things, but he did not wish to do so.

Alarmed, then irritated and troubled, attracted by Pelski to regions of brilliant dreams, and a splendid future of wealth, comfort, servants, and carriages, on the one side, on the other she rushed in mind to the modest lodgings of Yosef, inquiring anxiously why he did not come.

But he did not come. Pelski appeared every day more definitely as a rival. Lula, blaming Yosef for indifference, annoyed and humiliated by this, was willing, even through revenge, to give her hand to Pelski. Moreover, tradition attracted her in that direction. Who had the power, who ought to gain the victory, to foresee this was easy.

Pelski, in so far as he was able, strove to scatter the clouds from Lula's forehead, and frequently he succeeded in doing so. From time to time Lula had wonderful accesses of joyousness. She laughed then, and scattered

more or less witty words by thousands; and
though there was a kind of fever in this gladness, there was no little coquetry also. Her
eyes flashed on such occasions, from her temples there was a burning atmosphere. Her
lips played with an alluring smile; her words
wounded and fondled, attracted and repulsed
in turn. Pelski generally, and after a few unfortunate trials with Augustinovich, Pelski
alone, fell a victim to these freaks. He lost
his head then, and from the rôle of cousin protector he passed to that of a cousin captive.

And the more humble he became, the more
aggressive grew Lula; the sadder he was, the
gladder was she.

"Panna Malinka," whispered Augustinovich,
on such occasions, "never be like her; she is a
coquette."

"She is not," answered Malinka, sadly. "I
will remind you of these words."

It is difficult to say what Augustinovich
would have thought after such an evening, had
he seen that woman, who a moment before was
coquettish, left alone in her chamber, where
she sobbed so that long, long hours could not
quiet her.

The poor girl, she could not even confess
her suffering to any one, and the grievous bat-

tle which she was fighting all alone with herself. She wept in moments of weakness. How
much wounded self-love was there in those
tears, how much sincere love for Yosef, it is
difficult to tell. Formerly she would have put
her arms around the neck of the kind Malinka,
and confessed all that oppressed her soul, but
now even Malinka was a stranger to her, or at
least was not so near as formerly. Just those
unsuccessful attempts to coquet with Augustinovich had wounded deeply that maiden, who
was in love with him; and besides the relations
of Lula with Pelski seemed very odd to her.

Meanwhile time passed. Lula began to doubt
whether Yosef had ever loved her. Pelski
imperceptibly fed her with the thought of future
comfort. Time flowed on, and Time, according
to the words of the poet, " is the odious guardian
of blooming roses."

CHAPTER XVII

MALINKA tried frequently to learn of Augustinovich the real cause of Yosef's absence.

"Why bind her hands?" asked she, speaking of Lula.

Augustinovich assured her that he did not wish to bind Lula's hands, but afterward he was silent or lied.

On the other hand Yosef was convinced that the countess knew everything.

"I told her everything," said Augustinovich.

"But she? Do not hide from me!"

"Yosef?"

"What?"

"What is that to thee?"

Yosef gritted his teeth, but inquired no further. He was ashamed. He confessed to himself that those questions were an indulgence granted to weakness and to a former feeling. With consternation almost he saw that time had brought no relief. Oh, there were moments when he wished to cast away Helena and duty and conscience and go and sell even honor, even the remnant of self-respect, for one moment in which he could rest his head against the countess' shoulder. And he could not help meditating about her. So far he had conquered, but now he remembered that formerly he had been different from what he was then.

Formerly his character had that calm depth which concealed everything; to-day he boiled up. From passionate outbursts he passed frequently to melancholy and indifferent sentimentalism; he remembered how once he used to ridicule this in others, how he sneered without pity, how he despised even sentimentalism. Augustinovich knew this best of all.

A certain time (about a month after the breaking with Lula) Augustinovich, waking up late in the night, saw Yosef dressed yet and sitting with a book. The clock in the silent night told the fleeting moments untiringly. A lamp burnt with a clear, bright flame, and by its light the ruddy side whiskers and pale face of Yosef were outlined clearly on the black cover of the chair. He was sitting with head bent back and closed eyes, but he was not sleeping, his raised brows and the color of his face testified to this. His face had an expression of unspeakable bliss; some kind of dream, like a golden butterfly, was sitting on his brain and melting into misty mildness the sharp lines of his features.

Augustinovich looked at him carefully, then rose in the bed silently with a face full of indignation and anger. "What is he doing?" thought he. "Thou art tempting thyself! May I be hanged if I don't throw a pillow at thy head. Thou booby! Yes, I will throw the pillow! break the lamp — Hei!"

He had finished in a moment these warlike preparations, and was making ready to give the terrible blow, when he pushed under the blanket quickly; Yosef opened his eyes.

"I am curious to know what will happen now," muttered Augustinovich, pretending to sleep like a dead man. Meanwhile his astonishment grew in earnest.

Yosef looked at him suspiciously, then looked around like a criminal; finally he pulled out a drawer of the table and searched in it for some object.

"Ei! if he only does not want to shoot himself in the head, or poison himself," thought Augustinovich, terrified.

But Yosef had no thought of shooting or poisoning himself. The object which he drew forth was a glove. One small yellow wrinkled

glove. Ei! a poor little memorial, a historical
gift with which one says remember me. *Addio!
addio! caro mio!* Remember me. Yosef, like
that Emrod of old, would have gone for the
glove "among two leopards and a tiger for
it," but the question remained as to whether he
went away after that and never returned. In
point of stupidity the centuries agree oftener
than in sound judgment.

Yosef raised the glove to his lips.

"Be ashamed, old man!" roared Augustinovich.

In truth, there was something humiliating in
this, and afterward Yosef was greatly ashamed
of his act. Next morning he went out before
daylight to avoid Augustinovich, who was seriously angry and indignant. It seemed to him
that he had been deceived in Yosef.

"That dunce," said he, "is like others."
This idea roused that distaste in him which we
feel usually on beginning to lose regard for a
man whom we have thus far respected.

More important still was it that after that
event Augustinovich grew convinced that
Yosef would return to Lula. "Let the other
die or go mad," said he of the widow. "They
will take each other, let her die — Ei, let her
die" (Augustinovich always tried to persuade

himself that he did not like women), "there will be one less of them. Yosef will go back to Lula, he will."

He meditated then whether to tell Lula that Yosef was to marry, or not; in the end he resolved to be silent.

"But Helena is nothing to me. He will return to Lula; if I tell her everything it will be too late — it will be too late! Oh, ho, ho! But Helena too will lose, for again it will be too late. Yes, yes, I should not be able to correct the one, and should spoil the other. I shall say nothing, I will be silent — I will be silent."

He preferred Helena to Lula, a hundred times, and from his soul he preferred that Yosef should marry Helena; but he cared more for Yosef than for both women, therefore he wished Lula to be free "in every case." Besides, he considered that come what might, Lula would take Pelski. "Then," thought he, "I will tell the old man. 'Dost see,' I will say to him, 'I said nothing about Helena, she knew nothing about thy not loving her; still she married Pelski.'"

Finally, he concealed carefully the news of Yosef's intended marriage, in case that Lula, laughing and happy in view of Yosef's hypo-

thetical return, should give her hand to Pelski.
" Yosef will wish happiness to the lady, I will
say 'Crescite et multiplicamini!   He,' I shall
say, pointing to Yosef, 'has been betrothed this
long time; he loves and is loved immensely.' "

CHAPTER XVIII

DAYS passed, still Yosef did not return to the countess, but Malinka said to Augustinovich, —

"Pelski may offer himself any day to Lula."

"And if he does not, she may offer herself to him," answered Augustinovich, with emphasis.

"Oh, that is not true, not true."

"We shall see."

"No, Pan Adam. Lula has much womanly pride, and if she should marry Pelski it would be only through that same pride, through anger at Yosef's indifference. Besides, to tell the truth, Pelski is the only man who loves her, for he is the only one who has remained — on whom she can count."

"Ah! but evidently she likes to count on some one."

Malinka was angry.

"She counted once on Pan Yosef; she was deceived. How can you blame her, when he does not come — do you understand? — when he does not come?"

Pan Adam was silent.

"She has been deceived painfully," continued Malinka, "and believe me, I alone know what that costs her, and though we are not so friendly as before (she repulsed me herself), I see often how she suffers. Yesterday I went to her room and found her in tears. 'Lula!' asked I, though she withdrew from me, 'what is the matter with thee?' 'Nothing, I suffer from headache,' said she. 'My Lula,' said I, 'thou hast heartache, not headache!' I wished to throw myself on her neck, but she pushed me aside, and then stood up with such haughtiness that I was frightened. 'I was crying from shame,' said she, firmly. 'Wilt thou understand, from shame!' I wished to understand her, but was unable; I only know that the evening of that day I saw her in tears again. And dost thou see?"

"What does all this prove?"

"That it is not easy for her to renounce her idea of Yosef. What has happened that he does not come?"

"But if he should come?"

"She would not marry Pelski."

"Oh, I ridicule the idea that 'she would not.'"

"Yes, for you ridicule everything. But Pan

Yosef? Is it noble on his part to desert her in this way?"

"Who knows what he intends to do?"

"He ought to know himself," answered Malinka, decidedly, "and he should not conceal his intentions from her."

"He has no time, he is working."

That day, however, Malinka convinced herself that Yosef was not sitting so diligently at home as Augustinovich had represented. While walking with her mother, she met him passing with some young man. He did not notice them. Malinka was almost terrified at his appearance. He seemed to her as pale and crushed as if he had recovered from a grievous illness. "Then he has been sick," thought she, after returning home. Now she understood why Pan Adam would not explain the absence. "Yosef commanded him not to frighten Lula." All at once Yosef rose in Malinka's eyes to the loftiness of an ideal.

Augustinovich came in the evening, as usual. In the drawing-room Pani Visberg and the countess were present.

"Pan Adam," exclaimed Malinka, "I know why Pan Yosef has not been here for so long a time!"

Lula's eyes gleamed, but that moment she

controlled herself; still her hands trembled imperceptibly.

"The poor man, he must have been very sick; he is as pale as if he had come out of a coffin! Why did you not tell us of this?" asked Pani Visberg, quickly.

"Oh, Pan Adam was afraid that we should speak of it before Lula. Was that nice?" asked Malinka.

"What is the matter with thee, Lula? Art sick?"

"Nothing, nothing! I will come back in a moment."

Her face was pale, breath failed her. She went out, almost fled to her chamber. Pani Visberg wished to follow her. Malinka detained her gently but decisively.

"Thou must not go, mamma."

Then she turned to Augustinovich; her voice had a sad and serious sound.

"Pan Adam?"

Augustinovich bit his lips.

"Pan Adam! What is this? 'Lula is a coquette without a heart,' is she not?"

"Perhaps I was mistaken," blurted out Augustinovich; "but — but — "

He did not dare to cough out of himself at the moment that Yosef was going to marry Helena, that he would not come any more.

On returning home he was also afraid to tell Yosef what had happened.

Lula shut herself up in her chamber. Her head was on fire, and thoughts like a garland of sparks and ice were besieging her temples, and in the silence could be heard distinctly her hurried breathing and the throbbing of her heart. Pelski, Malinka, Pan Adam whirled around her in inexplicable chaos, and out of those fragments of thought as out of a grave rose higher and higher the pale, almost lifeless head of Yosef, with closed eyes. "He is sick! he is sick!" repeated she, in a whisper. "He will die, and never come here again."

Poor Lula interpreted differently from Malinka Yosef's absence. She judged that he had sacrificed himself for her, — that, not wishing to stand between her and Pelski, he had renounced her, and therefore he suffered so much and was sick. "Still, who told him that I should be happy with Pelski?" whispered she, quietly. "He did not trust me. My God, my God! but could he trust me?"

Memory brought before her as a reproach those moments of gleaming looks, alluring smiles, and velvety words given to Pelski; she remembered also that blush of shame with which she was blazing when Pelski learned that Yosef was the son of a blacksmith. And now she hid her burning face in her hands, but that was shame of another kind. It seemed to her at that moment that if Yosef himself were a blacksmith she would kiss his blackened forehead with delight even; even with perfect happiness would she place her head on his valiant breast, though it were covered with the apron of a blacksmith.

"How dark it is in my eyes! I did not know that I loved him," said she, trembling and aflame.

Her bosom moved quickly! Again some thought the most tender decked out her forehead with the brightness of an angel; she threw herself on her knees before an image of the Virgin.

"O mother of God!" cried she, aloud, "if any one has to suffer or to die, let me suffer, but preserve and love him, O Most Holy Mother!"

Then she rose in calmness, and was so bright with the light of love that one might have said that a silver lamp was shining in that dark little chamber before the image of the Holy Virgin.

During the two following days Augustinovich did not appear; but Pelski came, and according to Malinka's previsions, proposed to Lula. Seeing his cousin's face calm, and smiling with good hope, he expressed to her his hopes and wishes. The more painful was his astonishment when Lula gave him a decisively negative answer.

"I love another," was the substance of her answer.

Pelski wanted to learn who "that other" was. Lula told him without hesitation; then, as is done usually on such occasions, she offered him her friendship.

But Pelski did not accept the hand extended to him at parting.

"You have taken too much from me, you give me too little, cousin," whispered he, in a crushed voice. "For the happiness of a life-time — friendship !!"

But Lula felt no reproach after his departure. She was thinking of something else. This is the bad side of love, that it never thinks of anything but itself. It excludes particulars, but as a recompense includes the whole. Thou feelest that if the world were one man thou wouldst press him to thy bosom and kiss him on the head as a father.

Something like that did Lula feel when she went to Malinka's chamber after Pelski's visit. She needed to confess to some one all that lay on her heart.

Malinka was sitting near the window. In the twilight, on the darkened panes, could be seen her mild, thoughtful little face. All at once Lula's arms were clasped around her neck.

"Is that thou, Lula?" asked she, in a low voice.

"I, Malinka!" answered Lula.

She was sitting on a small stool near Malinka's feet; she put her head on her knees.

"My kind Malinka, thou art not angry with me now, and dost not despise me?"

Malinka fondled her like a child.

"I was very much to blame, as thou seest, but in my own heart I have found myself to-day. How pleasant it is for me here near thee! As formerly we talked long and often, let it be so to-day! Art thou willing?"

Malinka smiled half sadly, half jestingly, and answered, —

"Let it be so to-day, but later it will change. A certain 'His grace' will come and take Lula away, and I shall be left alone."

"But will he come?" inquired Lula, in a very low whisper.

"He will come. The poor man was sick surely from yearning. I did not understand what it meant that Pan Adam would not tell me why he came not; now I understand. Pan Yosef forbade him, he would not terrify thee."

"I think that he did not wish to hinder Pelski — so unkind of him to do this."

"But what did Pelski do?"

"I was just going to tell thee. He proposed to me to-day."

"And what?"

"I refused him, Malinka."

Silence continued awhile.

"He would not even take my hand when I gave it at parting, but could I do otherwise? I know that I acted very unkindly, very unkindly, but could I act otherwise? I do not love him."

"Better late than never. Thou didst obey the voice of thy heart. Only with Pan Yosef canst thou be happy."

"Oh, that is true, true."

"In a month or so," continued Malinka, "we shall array Lula in a white robe, weep over Lula the maiden and rejoice over Lula the wife. Thou wilt be happy, he and thou. He must be a good man, since all respect him so much."

"Do all respect him so much?" repeated Lula, who wanted to laugh and cry at the same moment.

"Oh, yes, mamma fears him even, and I also fear him a little, but I respect him for his character."

Lula put both hands under her head, and resting on Malinka's knees, looked into her face with eyes bright from tears.

Meanwhile it grew perfectly dark, then the moon rose, the dogs fell asleep; nothing was to be heard save the whispers of the two maidens filled with fancies by their talk.

All at once they were interrupted by the bell at the entrance.

"Maybe that is he!" cried Lula.

But it was not "he," for in the first room was heard Augustinovich's voice, —

"Are the ladies at home?"

"Go, Lula, into that room and hide there," said Malinka, quickly. "I will tell him how thou didst give the refusal to Pelski, I will beg him to repeat it to Pan Yosef. We shall see if he does not come. Thou mayst listen there."

The door opened. Augustinovich entered.

CHAPTER XIX

WE have said that Augustinovich feared to tell Yosef what had happened at Pani Visberg's. Lula had deceived his expectations; in spite of aristocracy, in spite of Pelski, she loved the young doctor, since news of his sickness had shocked her to such a degree.

Augustinovich lost his humor and the freedom of thought usual to him. Whether he would or not, he felt respect for Lula, and he felt respect for woman. Ei! that was something so strange in him, so out of harmony with his moral make up, that he could not come into agreement with himself. He had the look of a man caught in a falsehood, and the falsehood was his understanding of woman. He grew very gloomy. Once even (a wonderful thing and strange for him, or forgotten) words were forced from him that were full of painful bitterness: "Oh, if one like her could be met in a lifetime, a man would not be what he is." He avoided Yosef, he feared him, he hesitated, he wished to confess everything; then again he deferred it till the morrow.

Finally Yosef himself took note of his strange demeanor.

"What is the matter with thee, Adam?" asked he.

"But of Lula he cannot ask!" cried Augustinovich, with comical despair.

Yosef sprang to his feet.

"Of Lula? What does that mean? Speak!"

"It means nothing; what should it mean? Is all this to mean something right away?"

"Augustinovich, thou art hiding something?"

"But the fellow is thinking only of Lula!" cried Augustinovich, with increasing despair.

Yosef with unheard-of effort mastered himself, but that was a calm before a terrible storm. His sunken cheeks grew still paler, his eyes were flaming.

"Well, I will tell thee all!" cried Augustinovich, anticipating the outburst. "I will tell, I will tell! Ei, who will forbid me to tell thee that thou hast won the case! May Satan —— me if thou hast not won. She loves thee."

Yosef put his trembling hands to his perspiring face.

"But Pelski?" asked he.

"He has not proposed yet."

"Does she know everything about me?"

"Yosef!"

"Speak!"

"She knows nothing. I told her nothing."

Yosef's voice was dull and hoarse when he asked, —

"Why hast thou done me this injustice?"

"I thought that thou wouldst return to her."

Yosef twisted his hands till the fingers were cracking in their joints; Augustinovich's last words fell on him like red-hot coals. Return to her? That was to abandon Helena, and did not conscience itself defend Helena's cause? To return to Lula was to purchase the happiness of a lifetime, but to return to her was to dishonor Helena, to kill her, to become contemptible, to purchase contempt for himself. Oh, misfortune!

In Yosef's soul was taking place that devil's dance of a man with himself. Yosef was dancing with Yosef to the music of that orchestra of passion. Various thoughts, plans, methods, stormed in him; the battle raged along the whole line.

Augustinovich looked at his comrade with a face which was despairingly stupid, and he would have liked, as the saying is, to take himself by his own collar and throw himself out of doors.

All at once some decision was outlined on Yosef's face. The case was lost.

"Augustinovich!"

"What?"

"Thou wilt go this moment to Pani Visberg's and tell Lula that I am going to marry, that the ceremony will take place in a month, and that I never shall return to her, never. Dost understand?"

Augustinovich rose up and went.

Malinka received him in the way known to us. Lula was to hear their conversation from behind the door.

Malinka, full of imaginings from her recent talk with Lula, was gladsome and smiling; she pressed Pan Adam's hand cordially.

But he did not respond with a like cordiality.

"It is well that you have come," said she. "I have much to tell you, much."

"And I too have much to tell, much. I have come as an envoy."

"From Pan Yosef?"

"From Pan Yosef."

"Is he better?"

"He is sick. Has Pelski been here?"

"He has. I have wanted to talk of this."

"I am listening, Panna Malinka."

"He proposed to Lula."

" And what then? "

"She refused him. Oh, Pan Adam, she loves no man but Pan Yosef, she wants to belong to him only. My dear, honest Lula!"

Silence lasted a moment.

Pan Adam's voice quivered when he pronounced the following words deliberately, —

"She will not belong to him."

"Pan Adam!"

"Yosef, according to promise, is going to marry."

This news struck both young ladies like a thunderbolt. For a moment there was deep silence. All at once the door of the adjoining chamber opened. Lula entered the drawing-room.

On her face a blush of offended womanly dignity was playing, in her eyes pride was gleaming. It seemed to her that everything which she held sacred in her heart had been trampled.

"Malinka," cried she, "ask no more, I implore thee! Enough, enough! This gentleman has delivered his message. Why lower one's self by an answer?"

And taking Malinka by the hand, she led her out of the chamber almost with violence.

Augustinovich followed them awhile with his eyes, then nodded a couple of times.

"By the prophet!" said he, "I understand her. She is right, but so is Yosef. Hei! I must fly before everything breaks."

In a moment he ran to Pelski, told him the whole story.

"Some fatality weighed on them," concluded Augustinovich. "Yosef could not act otherwise, could he?"

"He acted as was fitting, but what inclined you to tell me of this?"

"A bagatelle. One question: Did not Lula act nobly in rejecting your hand?"

"I will leave the answer to myself."

"Leave it, my dear sir! The answer is all one to me, Lula is nothing to me; I know only that if my friend withdraws her future will not be enviable, and you are her cousin — The case is too bad."

Pelski thought awhile.

"Too bad? Ha, what is too bad?"

"That your proposal did not come a little later."

Pelski walked with quick step through the room.

"Now, never!" whispered he to himself.

Augustinovich heard this monologue.

"Too late, too late; but — but — now one small request. Tell no one that I was here, especially do not tell Pani Visberg or my friend if ever you see them."

"What is this to your friend?"

"Everything; but you would not understand it, dear count — Till our next meeting!"

Pelski, left alone, meditated long as to how that could really concern Augustinovich. He did not think out any answer, but came to the conviction that it might concern his own self somewhat.

"I might return to her, feigning ignorance of what has happened," said he. "Poor Lula!"

CHAPTER XX

THE two young ladies were sitting in Lula's chamber. That was a painful silence. If there are grievous moments in life, they had thrown their weight on the present fate of Lula. Everything which she held sacred in her breast had been trampled. She had put into that love the best parts of her moral existence, the victory to her had been like a wedding solemnity; by the power of this feeling she had risen from a momentary fall, she had conquered family prejudice, rejected the hand of a man who loved her, and with it a calm future, life in plenty, her own independence, and the pay for all this was information that he whom she loved was to marry another.

Ei! she lost still more. All the angelic qualities which preceding days had given her were crushed now into ruins of despair. Her soul might wither to its foundation! Had she not lost with love also faith and hope, not in their theological sense, but in all their vital value

for life? The ground was pushing from under
her. Like a boat without an oar, she was to
drift in the future beyond sight of shore.
To-day an orphan gathered in by honest
hearts, she may find herself to-morrow simply
suffering hunger, without a morsel of bread;
to-day so white that lilies might bloom on her
breast, she may in future stain that whiteness
with the gall of her own bitterness; to-day
half a child almost, in the spring, in the May
morning, she may after this or that number of
years have to look at her life's fruitless autumn.

Humiliated, broken, "like twigs after a tempest," pushed away from her moral basis, killed
in her happiness; with dry burning eyes she
pressed the weeping Malinka to her bosom
convulsively.

Lula did not weep, although she had tears
enough for weeping; anger had dried them.
But Malinka cried enough for both.

Next morning the countess received two
letters, — one from Pelski, the other from
Yosef.

"MADAME (wrote Pelski), — The pain which I
felt in consequence of your answer did not permit
me to reckon with my words. I rejected the friendship which you offered me. I regret that act. Though

I cannot explain your treatment of me, I see that you followed the voice of your heart. I trust that that voice has not deceived you. If he whom you have chosen loves you as much as I should, be assured of your happiness. I reproach him not, I dare not judge a man whom you love. As to myself, forced by stern necessity to part with the hope of possessing you, I implore you as the highest favor not to remember my words thrown out in a moment of pain. Permit me to return and claim that friendship inconsiderately rejected, friendship which for me in the future may take the place of the happiness of a lifetime."

In the evening Augustinovich brought a letter from Yosef. Lula did not wish to open it.

"Do not do him injustice," said Augustinovich, imploringly, "for at the present moment my old friend is perhaps —" Tears choked him, further words stuck in his throat. "These may be his last words — I took him to the hospital yesterday," whispered he.

Lula grew as pale as linen. It seemed for a moment that she would faint. In vain did she strive to preserve a calm and cool face, her whole body shook like a leaf. Come what might, she loved Yosef.

She took from Pan Adam's hand the letter, which read as follows: —

"DEAR LADY, — I was able to endure the loss of your hand, but not of your respect. Read and judge. A dying friend left to my care a woman whom he loved with all the power of a suffering heart. I had deprived him of the love of this woman without wishing to do so. After his death I became acquainted with her more intimately, and it seemed to me that I loved her. Unfortunately I told her so. After that you know, beloved lady, what happened. After that I hid from myself my ill-fated attachment to you. How much I suffered! Oh, pardon me! I am a man, I too must love, but still it was not from my lips that you learned of that love. When at last I stood before my own conscience, when the moment of memory came, judge yourself, how was I to act, whither was I to go, what was I to do? The oath to a dying man, the word given to a woman unhappy beyond expression, everything except my heart commanded me to abdicate you. It was not through my fault that you learned of this only yesterday. This news should have gone to you at the time when Count Pelski appeared. Misfortune, and the frivolity of a man ordained otherwise. This is the state of affairs! Judge, and, if you are able, forgive. Adam says that I am ill. This is true : my thoughts are weeping, I feel a burning in my blood, and out of pain and chaos I see one thing clearly, — that I love! that I love thee, O angel!"

After the reading of this letter the remnants of anger and pride vanished from Lula's forehead, on her beautiful face a mild though deep melancholy fixed itself.

"Pan Adam," said she, "tell the gentleman that he has acted as he should."

"And forgive me, dear lady," said Augustinovich, throwing himself on his knees. "I was unjust. I did you a wrong, but I had no idea, I knew not, that there were such women in the world as you are."

CHAPTER XXI

AUGUSTINOVICH went directly from Pani Visberg's to the hospital, where he remained all night. Yosef was ill, very ill. Typhus rushed at that strong organism, threatening it with utter destruction. About midnight the sick man began to rave; he talked with himself, and argued obstinately on the immortality of the soul with a black cat which he saw sitting on the bed. It appeared that he feared death, for a number of times indescribable terror was depicted on his face. He feared and trembled very acutely after every movement of Augustinovich. At moments he sang with a quivering voice, and as it were through sleep various gladsome and melancholy songs, or conversed with acquaintances. There was even a kind of astonishing humor in the naturalness of tones in these conversations.

Augustinovich, unmanned already by the events of preceding days, was irritated unspeakably. He waited for morning with longing, looking often at the window-panes, which, as if through spite, continued to be as black as ever. Outside there was deep darkness, and fine rain began to cut the window-panes, filling the hospital chamber with a sound which was monotonous and disagreeable.

For a long time such sad and disquieting thoughts had not wandered into Augustinovich's head as at that moment. Resting his elbows on his knees and covering his face with his hands, he meditated over the marvellous and painful complication of events during the last few days. Sometimes he raised his head and cast a quick glance at the sick man; at times it seemed to him that the gloom of death was falling on the withered, sharp features of Yosef.

Augustinovich pondered over this, how a man, so active and broadly living a short time before, would be in a couple of days, perhaps, something dead, which they would bury in the ground, and the comedy would be ended! Oh, an ordinary, every-day thought, and every day equally bitter for those who must think: This is the end! dust! Still, when he lived with full life, he judged, analyzed, acted perhaps more widely than others. As a plough turns out the sod, so he, in the soil of life, from the furrows of good and evil was

winning good and — ? Involuntarily one asks
for the moral sense of this fable. Where,
when, on what planets, will living persons find
an answer beyond the tomb? Immortality?
— In the ocean of human acts perhaps a few
moral atoms of the deeds of the dead survive,
but that *I*, powerful, energetically self-conscious, where is it? And those atoms of acts
are like the corpse of a sailor dropped down
from a ship into the abyss of the sea. Where
shall we look for them, and who will find them?
Will God ever fish them out from those shoreless billows, and will He develop from them
a new self-conscious being? "*È bene trovato!*"
The bitterness of these thoughts settled now
on the sleepy forehead of Augustinovich, but
meanwhile the window-panes from black began
to turn gray. It was dawning. In the chamber
the light of the candle grew rosier gradually
and fainter, objects began to issue from the
shade. In the corridors were heard now the
steps of the hospital servants. An hour later
the doctor came in.

"How is the patient?" inquired he.

"Ill," answered Augustinovich, abruptly.

The doctor thrust out his lower lip with importance, wrinkled his forehead, and felt the
pulse of the sick man.

"What do you think?" inquired Augustinovich.

"Well, what? I think nothing — he is ill, very ill."

A shade of irony passed over Augustinovich's face.

"But I think, professor, that medicine is a very dull child which believes that if it takes its heels in its hands it can lift itself. Is this not the case?"

The doctor nodded a couple of times, prescribed some cooling medicine, and went out. Augustinovich, looking at the prescription, shook his head in his turn, shrugged his shoulders, and sat at the bed.

Meanwhile the patient grew worse toward evening, about midnight he was almost dying. Augustinovich wept like a child and knocked himself against the walls of the chamber. He sat up again through the whole night.

Toward morning it seemed to him that he noticed a slight improvement, but that improvement was deceptive. Pale and red spots appeared on the sick man; evidently he had burnt out in fever and was quenching.

In the evening Pani Visberg came. Augustinovich would not admit her to the room. From his face she learned that something terrible must be happening.

"Is he alive?" cried she.

"He is dying!" answered Augustinovich, briefly.

A few hours later the chaplain of the hospital anointed Yosef. Augustinovich had not strength to be present at the ceremony; he ran out into the city.

He needed to collect his thoughts, he needed to draw breath; he felt that his thoughts were beginning to grow dim — very likely the loss of Yosef would destroy his balance. He had expected everything, but not that Yosef would die.

He did not know himself whither he was hurrying; a number of times he halted as if in fear that he would return too late.

All at once some thought flashed through his head; he noticed that he was standing before Helena's lodgings.

"I will go in. Let her take farewell of him!"

Half an hour later Helena was kneeling at Yosef's bed. Her unbound hair was lying in broad tresses on the bed; she was embracing the sick man's feet with her hands, her face resting on them.

In that room of the hospital reigned a silence of the grave; nothing was heard but the quick broken breath of Yosef.

So passed the long, cursed night, every moment of which seemed the last one for Yosef. Finally, on the thirteenth day from the first the disease was vanquished. Yosef was decidedly better.

At his bed sat, without leaving it, Augustino-vich and Helena; the latter seemed to forget the world at that bed. With Yosef's life life returned to Helena also. She was delighted to ecstasy with even the smallest proof of improvement.

At last Yosef regained consciousness.

Augustinovich was not present at that moment; the first person whom he saw was Helena.

The sick man looked at her for a moment; on his forehead a certain working of thought became evident.

At last he recalled her to mind. He smiled. Evidently the smile was forced; still Helena threw herself on her knees with tears of delight.

But Augustinovich when he returned noticed that her presence disquieted the sick man and even tortured him. Yosef did not take his eyes from Helena for an instant; he followed every movement of hers.

With that inane gesticulation peculiar to old or to sick people he moved his lips.

Augustinovich followed Yosef's eyes carefully. He had a foreboding of evil.

Meanwhile, as usual, toward evening the fever increased; still the sick man fell asleep. Augustinovich strove to persuade Helena to go home for rest.

"I will not leave him for a moment," answered she, with what for her was uncommon decision.

Augustinovich took his seat in the armchair in silence and meditated deeply; soon his head began to weigh on him, his lids became leaden, an invincible drowsiness seized him with increasing force, his head dropped on his breast, he nodded to the right, to the left, and fell asleep.

After a while he woke again.

"Is he sleeping?" inquired he, looking at Yosef.

"He is sleeping, but unquietly," answered Helena.

Augustinovich again dropped his head. Suddenly a shriek from Helena roused him.

The sick man was sitting up in bed in a paroxysm of malignant fever; his face was burning, his eyes glittering like those of a wolf; his emaciated hand was extended toward Helena.

"What is this!" cried Augustinovich.

Helena seized him convulsively by the hands; she felt that his whole body trembled.

"Do not torture me!" whispered the sick man, with a hoarse, broken voice. "Thou hast killed Gustav, and now thou wouldst kill me. Away! I do not love thee! Be off!"

Again he fell on the bed.

"Lula, my Lula, save me!" whispered Yosef.

Augustinovich almost by force conducted Helena from the chamber. In the corridor was heard for a while quick conversation, and the name of the countess was repeated. At last Augustinovich returned alone.

He was pale, great drops of sweat were flowing down his forehead.

"Everything is ended now," said he, in a whisper.

Helena ran driven by despair. Yosef's words and the brief conversation with Augustinovich had cleared as with a bloody lightning-flash many circumstances which had been dark to her. She ran with the single object of going straight forward. Her thoughts were burning her like fire, or rather they were thoughts no longer, they were a circle of fire sparks driven around madly by a whirlwind.

The city in that evening hour was lighted with a thousand lamps, calm domestic fires looked through the clear windows at her. She ran on. Through the streets throngs of people flowed forward as usual; some passers-by turned around to gaze at her; one young man said something with a smile, but looking her in the eyes he drew back in fright. She ran on. At last instead of streets there were alleys, next alleys which were emptier and darker. In the windows lights were evident no longer; there the wearied population were sleeping after the toil of the day; in a rare place a lamp gleamed, or the echoes of a foot-step were heard.

The night was damp, but calm; a kind of weight oppressive to the spirit was hanging in the atmosphere. From the Dnieper came a harsh breeze; a watery mist left drops on Helena's clothing and hair. On, on she ran. Nervous spasms distorted her face. In spite of the coolness it seemed to her that fire from heaven was falling on her head, her hands, and her breast. Those little fires seemed to dance and whirl about her, and in each one of them she saw the face now of Yosef, now of Gustav. Her cape had fallen off, the wind had torn her hat away, dampness unbound her hair. She fell to the earth a number of times. Soon amid night and emptiness she found herself alone. Only the distant noise of the city and the barking of dogs in that part through which she was hastening pursued her. She ran ever forward.

She felt neither torture nor pain. All her thoughts rushed to one centre; that was her misfortune. When love takes a part of one's life, it pays with disappointment; for Helena love had been everything. Existence for her had ceased now to have sense. The charm was broken. There was no forgiveness for that woman, though she had "loved much;" there could be only peace, not in life, but beyond it.

Meanwhile she ran forward, but strength was deserting her. Her lips had grown parched, her eyes were now dim, her clothing wet and bespattered with mud. She fell oftener and oftener; sometimes she turned her face to the sky, seizing the air greedily. The ground on which she was running became wetter and wetter. From afar could be heard now the sobbing of the wave, and that marvellous converse of water, half fitful, half gloomy.

At the brink Helena halted a moment.

Closing her eyes on a sudden and stretching

her hands out before her, the woman rushed forward.

With the plash in the river was heard a short scream, stopped by the water, — her last scream.

Then followed silence. Deep night was in the sky.

CHAPTER XXII

"EVERYTHING is marvellously involved in this poor world," said the ancient poet. This is certain, that more than once life becomes so involved that it is only to be cut like that Gordian knot of old. So was it with Yosef.

A few years before he had come to Kieff full of confidence in his own strength. It had seemed to him that he could push forward not only his own fate, but that of others in a way chosen in advance. Meanwhile he had convinced himself that in a short time he had lost the rudder even of his own boat. He had been left to rush and save himself if he wished, but he had to sail with the wind, and therewith he had little happiness in life. In his case, as in that of all men, life, or rather the excess of that seething of youthful years, had to pour out in the single but very narrow direction of love for woman. There was little space between the banks; hence the stream flowed too violently, so that in all Yosef's past there were barely a few peaceful moments. He lacked little of paying with his life for the past, and God knows there was nothing to pay for. After the last incident with Helena the danger might be renewed. Augustinovich feared relapse ; happily his fears were not justified.

Yosef improved continually. It was difficult to foresee how long he would have to lie in bed yet ; his weakness after the grievous illness was very great, but his return to health was assured.

Augustinovich shortened the long hospital hours to the best of his power and ability, but vain were his efforts to win back the old-time humor. Recent events had made him sedate and sparing of words. He had lost many of his old habits. From the time of Yosef's illness he had not visited Pani Visberg even once, though she came rather often to inquire for Yosef's health.

But if in this way events of recent days had acted on Augustinovich, how much more had they acted on Yosef! Out of his long illness he rose a new man altogether. He had no longer that lively, active, unbending temperament. In his movements there was slowness, in his look heaviness, and as it were indolence.

Augustinovich attributed this, and justly, to the weakness unavoidable after such an illness.

but soon he noticed in the sick man other
things foreign to him before. A certain marvellous indifference approaching apathy broke
through his words. He began to look at the
world again, but in a manner entirely different
from that in which he had looked at it earlier.
He seemed to be capable of no vivacious feeling. It was disagreeable to look at him; these
changes had touched not merely his moral side,
he had changed physically also. His hair had
grown thin, his face was white and emaciated,
his eyes had a sleepy look, he had lost his
former brightness. Lying whole days without
movement, he looked for hours together at
one point in the ceiling, or slept. The presence of any one did not seem to concern him.

All this alarmed Augustinovich, especially
when he considered that in spite of the speedy
return of physical strength these symptoms, if
they yielded, yielded very slowly. He sighed
when he remembered the former Yosef, and
he labored to rouse the present one, but the
labor was difficult.

A certain time Augustinovich, sitting by the
bed of the sick man, read aloud to him. Yosef
was lying on his back; according to habit he
was looking at the ceiling. Evidently he was
thinking of something else, or was thinking of

nothing, for after a certain time annoyance was expressed on his face. Augustinovich stopped reading.

"Dost wish to sleep?"

"No, but the book wearies me."

Augustinovich was reading "Dame aux Camélias."

"Still, there is life and truth here."

"Yes, but there is not judgment to the value of a copper."

"Still, the book raises the question of such women!"

"But whom do such women concern?"

"They once concerned thee."

Yosef said nothing; on his face a slight thoughtfulness was evident.

After a time he asked,—

"What is happening with Helena? Has she been here?"

Augustinovich was confused.

"She has been here, she has been here."

"Well, and now?"

"That is—yes—she is sick, very sick."

Yosef's face continued indifferent.

"What is the matter with her?" asked he, leisurely.

"With her?—She—Well, I will tell thee the truth, only be not frightened."

"Well?"

"Helena is no longer alive — she was drowned."

Some sort of indefinite impression shot over Yosef's face; he made an effort as if to rise in the bed, but after a while he dropped his head on the pillow.

"By accident or design?" asked he.

"Rest, old man, rest; it is not permitted thee to talk much. Later I will tell everything."

Yosef turned to the wall and sank into silence. At that moment a servant of the hospital entered.

"Pani Visberg wishes to see you," said he to Augustinovich.

Augustinovich went out; in the corridor Pani Visberg was waiting.

"What has happened?" inquired he, with concern. "Is some one sick?"

"No, no!"

"What then?"

"Lula has gone away!" said Pani Visberg, in a sad voice.

"Long ago?"

"Yesterday evening. I should have come here at once, for during the whole week I had not heard from Yosef, but Malinka was so afflicted, and had cried so much that I could not let her come. Lula has gone, she has gone!"

"Why did she go?"

"It is difficult to tell. Maybe two weeks from the time that Yosef fell ill, Pelski came again, and soon after proposed to her a second time. She experienced no small suffering from that, for evidently the little man had become attached to her seriously. Still she refused him, giving as cause that she could not marry without attachment. I liked that Pelski well enough. But that is not the point! The honest girl refused him, naturally. How much she suffered during Yosef's sickness! But that again is not the point. She and Pelski parted without anger, and he undoubtedly found her that place in Odessa. Imagine to yourself my astonishment when a few days ago she came to me and declared that Yosef's illness was all that had delayed her departure, that now, when he was better, she would not be a burden on me longer, that she wanted to work for a morsel of bread, and would go. But, my God! was she a burden to me? Malinka became educated and acquired polish in her society; besides, I loved her."

Augustinovich thought awhile; only after long silence did he say, —

"No, kind lady! I understand Lula. When she took lodgings with you she was a spoiled and capricious young girl, who thought that you were receiving her for her coronet, and to be honored yourself; to-day she is quite different."

"Do I reproach her with anything?" asked Pani Visberg.

"That is not a question. I understand how bitter it must have been for you and your daughter to part with her, and it is too bad that you did not let me know of this before. The person whom Yosef was to marry is no longer alive."

"No longer alive?"

"She is not. But except pain for you, this departure will cause no harm. Yosef has not passed examination for his medical degree; he must think of that first of all, for it is his bread. When he recovers and assures a sustenance for himself, he will go to Odessa after her, but for that time is needed. Yosef has changed very much. It is no harm that Lula has done everything that can raise her still more in his esteem."

Pani Visberg went away with a straitened heart. Augustinovich stood awhile on one spot, then he shook himself from his meditation and took on a gloomy look.

"She has rejected Pelski a second time," thought he; "she wants to work for her living! Oh, Yosef, Yosef! even to go through greater suffering than thine — "

He did not finish the thought which he had begun; he waved his hand, and went to the chamber.

"What did Pani Visberg want?" asked Yosef, with an apathetic voice.

"Lula has gone to Odessa," answered Augustinovich, abruptly.

Yosef closed his eyes and remained motionless a long time, At last he said, —

"It is a pity! That was a good girl — Lula."

Augustinovich gritted his teeth and made no answer.

The time came at last when Yosef left the hospital, and a month later he passed his examination as doctor of medicine. It was a clear autumnal day. The two friends, with their diplomas in their pockets, were returning to the house. Yosef's face bore on it yet the marks of disease, but otherwise he was perfectly healthy. Augustinovich walked arm in arm with him; along the road they talked of the past.

"Let us sit here on this bench," said Augustinovich when they entered the garden. "It is a beautiful day, I like to warm myself in the sun on such a day."

They sat down. Augustinovich stretched himself comfortably, drew a long breath, and said with gladsome feeling, —

"Well, old man! we ought to have had in our pockets for the last three months these wretched rolls which we have received only to-day."

"True," replied Yosef, pushing away with his cane a few yellow leaves that were lying at the side of the bench.

"The leaves are falling from the trees, and the birds are moving southward," said Augustinovich. Then lowering his voice and pointing to a flock of wagtails flying above the trees, he added, —

"But wilt thou not go south after the couriers of the sun?"

"I? Whither?"

"To the Black Sea — to Odessa."

Yosef bent, and remained silent for a long time, then he raised his head; on his face was depicted something almost like despair.

"I love her no longer, Adam!" whispered he.

On the evening of that day Augustinovich said to Yosef, —

"We put too much energy into chasing after woman's love; later on that love flies away like a bird, and our energy is wasted."